The Ghostwriter

Sarah Sheridan

First published in 2023 by Bloodhound Books.

www.bloodhoundbooks.com

Print ISBN: 978-1-5040-8248-8

Also by Sarah Sheridan

The Sister Veronica Mysteries:

The Convent (book one)

The Disciple (book two)

The Tormented (book three)

Devil's Play

Girl in Bed Three

A Perfect Family

The Temptress (novella)

For my amazing friend Erin

Chapter One

It was my sister, Marie, who introduced me to Sylvie Kaminski. We've always been close, me and Marie. She looked out for me when we were little, she was bigger in size as well as age, then as now. I'm the family runt, small and skinny, with lank blonde hair rather than the glowing chestnut mop that my sister got from our mum. We're like chalk and cheese, but we're incredibly tight-knit, all the same. Not in a lovey, huggy kind of way, more in a 'I'll always have your back' sense.

I'd been complaining to Marie for a while about how my work as a ghostwriter had all but dried up since the rush before Christmas – it was now mid-March – how I had bills to pay and my six-year-old son, Danny, to feed. The company that I was signed up with – UK Ghostwriting Team – had stopped sending so many enquiries through. I wasn't sure why, maybe they'd taken on more and more writers and had to disperse work more widely. Or perhaps someone had complained about something I'd written. Who knows? I was a single mum, I had no one else to rely on to look after Danny, so I was reluctant to look for a full-time job because it would mean I'd hardly see him. My best friend, Brigitte – who I'd been close with ever since we'd met during my first term at the University of London – had decided to move back to France last year, a change that had hit me hard. I really missed her, and we often emailed and texted, but it wasn't the same as having her living round the corner. Now I thought of Marie as my best mate – in this country, at least.

Danny and I were each other's everything. I desperately wanted to keep working from home, as I knew his childhood years would pass quickly and I wanted to be there for them, but that was looking more and more unlikely. All I knew was that I was down to my last two hundred quid and worried out of my mind, with red letter bills coming through the door daily, when my sister rang me that early spring morning, just after I was back from the school run.

'Polly,' she'd said, an excited tone in her voice. 'Guess what? I think I've found you a new customer. Fresh meat. And from the car she drives, I know she can afford it too.'

'Really?' I said, sitting down at the kitchen table. 'Who?' I'd learnt the hard way that it was important to make sure that potential clients had the means to pay for their books before I started writing them. The UK Ghostwriting Team got quite a few enquiries through from people who wanted us to work for free. 'Just send me a sample,' they'd say. Or, 'Write the book for me and I'll give you a share of the royalties'. Nope, that wasn't how I did things. I asked for a down payment of two hundred pounds, to make sure that the new client could a) afford to pay me, and b) was invested in the project. And then after that, I arranged with them that they would pay me in instalments; one hundred pounds for every three thousand words written. I never wanted to get into the situation where I spent weeks putting together someone's novel, only to find that they couldn't pay for it after all. My confidence in myself as a writer had really grown over the last few years – especially since the bestseller – and I now realised that I wasn't at all bad at what I did. I may not be the next Tolkien or Shakespeare, but I now understood that I could put together a pretty decent book for someone. And the book I'd written for the army vet about his time serving, that had stayed in the top UK one hundred for more than a month, was proof of this. So if Marie had found a person who could pay me to do this for them, then I was all ears...

'I'm friendly with a lady called Sylvie,' Marie was saying. 'Sylvie Kaminski. She's one of the mums at Oliver and Bella's school. Oh my God, Polly, you seriously won't be able to believe your ears when you hear the story that she's got to tell. It's insane. I barely believed her until she brought up news reports about it on her phone. Do you want me to give you her number? I said I'd tell you all about her, and that you'd probably be in contact. I've already promoted you to the max, and told her you're a bestselling ghostwriter.'

'Wow, yes of course, thanks, Marie,' I said, staring around at my messy kitchen surfaces for a pen. Keeping the place tidy had never been my forte, but I actually preferred our house to look comfortable and homely, rather than show-home ultra-tidy. For some reason it made me feel more relaxed. I could hardly believe what my sister was saying. *Could this really be happening? A potential new client with a great story to tell? This honestly couldn't have come at a better time...*

I located a biro and scribbled down Sylvie's number on the back of yet another reminder to pay my electricity bill.

Marie and I chatted on for a while after that. Her kids went to a private school, whereas Danny went to the local Church of England one at the bottom of our road. Marie's husband, Henry, was some sort of big shot in South Western Banking. I've never really understood exactly what his role was there; all I knew was that Marie hadn't had to work since she married him, and she could not only afford to send Oliver and Bella to Aston Bennett's, the best private school around, but they could also afford regular amazing holidays, as well as to keep updating their cars every few years. While she was technically 'at home' all day, Marie wasn't someone I could foist Danny onto for childcare. Her children did a trillion after-school clubs, and she'd never have time to drop him off or pick him up if I had to take on a 'proper' job, working for someone else. Which made my plan to continue working from home as a writer all the more important...

I didn't begrudge Marie any of her luxurious lifestyle at all. I've always looked up to her, and regarded her as my best friend and confidante. She'd been there for me when my relationship with Danny's father – Jakub – had fallen apart all those years ago. She'd supported me financially when I'd been at breaking point, she'd handed down old clothes that Oliver had grown out of when I couldn't afford to buy my son outfits that he so desperately needed. She'd been the strong one when Mum had passed away five years ago, after her horrendously painful battle with cancer. Dad had gone even more into himself since then, I'd always known that he'd loved my sister and I, but his affection felt increasingly distant. It was as though he was nearly ready to give up and call it a day himself... All in all, Marie had been an absolute star.

And I've never really been materialistic; I'm very happy with the tiny two-bed cottage that I own – with a mortgage – in Penge, South London, and my old, shabby Nissan Note. Yes, I don't lead a flashy lifestyle, nothing like the one that Marie and Henry live twenty minutes away in the expensive part of Beckenham, with their dinner parties and posh friends. But Danny and I have everything we need, and even though we just scrape by sometimes and have eaten beans on toast more times than I can remember, I can still just about manage to give us the life that we need. And when Danny's at school, I get a chance to write my own, precious crime novels, when I'm not working on someone else's book. I'm still waiting for my big break with them, I'd love one of them to be a top one hundred bestseller too, but I have a feeling that one will come along one day if I can just keep coming up with ideas. My secret ambition is to get a place on the much esteemed creative crime-fiction writing course that the Open University run. I have a feeling that if I do that, I'll unlock some kind of inner floodgates that will help me pour my ideas onto paper. The amount of times I've perused that internet page is unreal. The only problem is that I can't afford it, it's over two grand. But if I could just save up the money...

'You wouldn't believe the fuss that Anna, Sebastian's mum, made about hot dog day last week,' Marie was saying, while I was daydreaming about the possibility of taking on Sylvie as a new client. 'Honestly, the woman's new to the school, her son has only been there a term. But suddenly she joins the PTA, and starts banging on about the importance of giving the kids a nourishing treat rather than hot dogs on the PTA fundraising day. They all love hot dog day! Christ, it's not as though they're eating shit in a bun. Well, not exactly...'

I smiled as I leaned back on the wooden chair. Marie's always been much more outspoken than me. She's the extrovert, like Mum was. I'm much more introverted, like Dad. I'd never have the guts to stand up to someone like this Anna that Marie was describing, whereas my sister most definitely would. Although, to be fair, the old Polly – the one who was younger and hadn't been worn down by the strains of single-parentdom – had been a lot more feisty. More likely to stand up for herself. I was just inwardly very tired now. But I'm always secretly hoping that I'll get some of that sparky assertiveness back one day...

'So I decided to make a petition,' Marie was saying. 'Asking parents who wanted to keep hot dog day and who wanted it abolished in favour of some disgustingly nutritious vegan day. Of course, the hot dogs won hands down...'

Yep, I thought. *That was Marie all over. Take the bull by the horns, and fight every battle with the intention of winning. Which, of course, she usually did.*

'I've got to dash now,' Marie said. 'Bella's doing a ballet performance this evening, and I need to get her outfit together. It's *Midsummer Night's Dream*, and she's playing Titania. But now you've got Sylvie's number, do give her a ring, Polly. I promise you won't be disappointed with what she's got to tell you. And let me know how you get on, okay?'

'I will,' I said. 'And thanks so much for this, Marie. I really owe you one.'

We said our goodbyes and I thought for a minute, and then quickly fired off a text to Sylvie, explaining that I'd just heard from my sister, and asking if she'd like to meet for a drink and a chat about the potential book.

But as I laid my phone down on the table, a contented smile spreading across my face. I had absolutely no idea what I was about to take on. Of the world that I was so unwittingly going to stumble smack bang into. And of the enormous danger I was about to bring upon not only myself, but my son Danny as well...

Chapter Two

The butterflies in my stomach swirled around more intensely as I pushed open the door to Babka Eatery on Beckenham High Street, the March sunshine on my face. Sylvie had texted me back within minutes of receiving my message yesterday, and had said that she'd love to meet up – the earlier the better, she said – and suggested we chat at the bistro she ran. We'd made arrangements for the following day, and I'd spent the rest of the evening vacillating between excitement and nerves. I so badly needed this project to work out, and I wanted to make sure I came across as professional and competent as possible. So on a whim, I sent Sylvie another message, asking for her email address. When she sent it over minutes later, I pinged her through my CV, links to the anthologies that I'd had short crime stories published in, information about the ghostwriting company I worked for, and also a link to the gorgeous little article that the local paper had written about me a couple of years before, after one of the anthologies I'd contributed to had had some significant success. And of course, I made sure to let her know that I'd penned the bestselling book by the army war veteran – I mean, I'd have been stupid not to...

It looked like quite a classy place, I decided, as I stared around at the polished tables and beautiful flowery prints on the walls. It was midday, and already quite full of customers, and their murmurs and laughter filled the air around me, putting me slightly more at ease. I'd done a bit of internet research on Sylvie and Babka Eatery before leaving the house, and had found out that she was born in Poland and grown up helping out in her parents' café, but had lived in England for ages. She'd set up the bistro quite a few years ago, and it had an impressive amount of four- and five-star reviews on Google.

'Polly Manning?' a voice called, and I turned to see a slender, beautiful woman coming through a door at the back of the restaurant. 'I'm Sylvie, it's so nice of you to come and see me.' Her words had a gentle accent to them, but she was obviously completely fluent in English, which was fantastic as it would really help communication between us. I'd found with my previous clients that to really pick up on the heart of their life stories, I had to listen to every nuance and inflection in what they said, as well as hearing what they *weren't* saying – what they left out – in order to gain a solid understanding of where they'd come from and what they'd been through.

'Hi,' I called, waving. I've always been a bit shy if I'm honest, which I tend to put down to my natural introversion. Sometimes I'm not very good at small talk, and for a brief second a wave of fear flooded through me, because the reality of the fact that I was meeting this new, glamorous potential client hit me in the face, and for a moment I felt like a nervous teenager. *What if I fuck it all up? What if I don't get this job? Come on, Polly*, I told myself. *You've got to pull this one out of the bag. Don't be shy today. Be the confident writer that you are. You can do this. Channel the old feistiness that you used to have, it must still be in you somewhere...*

As she approached, I saw that Sylvie's face had a gritty,

almost hard look about it. Like she'd lived through her own fair share of traumatic times, and then some. But when she smiled her features transformed, and I found myself smiling back at her without any hesitation at all.

'It's lovely to meet you, Sylvie,' I said, offering her my hand, which she shook immediately.

'I've saved us the booth at the back,' Sylvie said, turning and pointing to a secluded area at the rear of the restaurant. 'And my staff are under strict instructions not to disturb us until we've finished chatting. Come, let me get you a drink and something to eat first. It's on the house, choose anything you want, please.'

A few minutes later, after I'd hurriedly perused the menu she'd handed me and chosen a cappuccino and some fried sauerkraut, we were both nestled in the booth. Sylvie was staring at me intently.

'Polly,' she said. 'I have a very big story to tell you. And I have evidence for everything in it, which I know is important as Marie, bless her, didn't believe half of what I was saying until I showed her the news reports. Please don't take offence at this, but I need to ask you if you will keep everything I say confidential. I know I will have to change the names of some of the people involved, and I am going to have the book published under a different name, definitely not under my own. I really don't want word to get out about what I am doing. But I have lived this truth for a very long time now, and I need to tell my version of everything that happened. It will be a release for me. But please, only Marie – and in a minute you – will know that it is me telling this story.'

'Of course,' I said, nodding. 'Everything you tell me will be kept entirely confidential, and we can sign a confidentiality agreement together in order to protect everything you say.' This was a fairly typical request from clients, as I'd discovered during my seven years of ghostwriting. Older clients who wanted to write their memoirs were usually more than happy to put their names on the covers of their books. But younger ones – with more complicated life experiences – often wanted to use pen names, for a variety of reasons. And I totally respected the choices of each person I worked with. I simply saw myself as their human typewriter; I was enabling them to write down the words that they felt compelled to tell the world about.

'Thank you,' Sylvie said, her shoulders visibly relaxing.

I reached into my handbag and pulled out my Dictaphone.

'Would it be okay if I recorded everything we chat about today?' I said. 'If we agree to go forward together with this project, then everything we talk about will be really useful and help me get started with the book.' It was something I did with everyone I worked with, no matter whether we were chatting over video call, phone or in person. You never knew when a gem of information would arise, and with my memory having gone down the pan since having Danny, I found the recordings the best and most reliable source to work from.

'Absolutely,' Sylvie said, with a quick smile. She watched as I turned on the gadget, and then checked it was working all right. I placed it on the table, halfway between the two of us. 'So now, I'll begin. Hold on to your seat, Polly...'

Chapter Three

I leaned forward, listening intently, as Sylvie talked.

'I've known Antoni for years,' she was saying. 'We grew up in Podlaskie Voivodeship in Poland together, in Gruszki village. He was a bad boy back then, but nothing like the person he is today. Neither of our families had much money, mine owned a café and managed to scrape enough together to get by. But his father had left the family, and his mother struggled a lot, trying to feed her seven children.'

I nodded. Sylvie sighed.

'When I was thirteen and Antoni was fourteen, we were both part of the same friendship group. In the evenings, the whole lot of us would just hang around together, finding places to smoke weed and have a laugh. Then Antoni and his mates started the stealing. He'd never had much, you see, so when he realised he could get better clothes by just taking them from someone else rather than working for them, he was so happy. I didn't approve of this behaviour one bit. But there was just something about him, the way his eyes looked when he smiled, that drew me to him...'

She stopped and shook her head.

'We ended up dating. My parents were furious about it, they hated Antoni as they knew he was getting in trouble with the police. But I used to find ways to get out of the house and go and see him when they'd grounded me. I was also a bit of a wild child back then, but nothing like him. Anyway, we were together for about three years. But then I found out that he was cheating on me, and I ended it. Which is when I saw his true temper for the first time. He found out where I was and came and screamed and shouted in my face, telling me that I was making a big mistake. But I'd made up my mind to move on. I can be quite stubborn sometimes, you know? So that was that. Two years later, when I was eighteen, I had the chance to move to England to stay with some friends of my parents. They'd come over here years before, and set up quite a successful cleaning business. They live in Crystal Palace.'

I nodded. I knew it well, it was just up the road from where I lived in Penge.

'I've been here ever since, apart from the odd trip back to Poland to see my family. And I'd completely moved on from Antoni. At least that's what I thought. Because one day, after I'd been here for about three years, I got a phone call and it was him. He said he'd moved to England too, and that someone had given him my number. He asked if we could meet, said it would be good to see a friendly face as he was feeling a bit lonely. Despite my better judgement I said yes...'

Sylvie paused.

'We met in The Old Oak pub in Sydenham, which was near where he was sharing a house with five other Polish men,' she went on. 'I was twenty-one at that point, and I hadn't seen Antoni for five years. I couldn't believe how much he'd changed. His eyes were hard, like the light in them had gone out. He was ripped, so muscly, and was covered in tattoos. But after a few drinks, I could feel that chemistry between us returning. And he was so sweet to me. If I'm honest, Polly, I'd also been feeling a bit lonely. All I did was work, and spend time with the Dabrowskis, the family I was working for. I missed having fun. So after that we became a couple again.'

Sylvie stopped and looked down at her hands.

'Getting back together with Antoni was the biggest mistake I've made in my life,' she said. 'He's a bad, bad person. He's so deluded, he's almost insane. But I couldn't see that then. I was blinded by what I felt for him, and how protected he made me feel. To start with, anyway. I used to ask him what he did for work, as he always had so much spare cash. To begin with, he told me he did labouring jobs, worked on building sites and stuff.

'But then one day, I found a packet of white powder in his jacket pocket. I asked him what it was, and he told me it was cocaine. That it helped him stay awake when he was working long hours. I chose to believe him, because I felt happy at that stage and I didn't want anything to spoil our relationship. Once, we were out in his car, and he suddenly pulled over to the side of the road. A man came up and leaned through the driver's window. I literally couldn't believe my eyes, but I then watched Antoni pull a small plastic bag out of his pocket and pass it to the man. The man then gave him some money. Antoni wound his window up, and we drove off. "What the fuck did you do that for?" I shouted at him. "Are you a drug dealer?" It turned out that he was. And after I found out what he was up to, Antoni's behaviour towards me began to change.

'We'd just moved in together at that point, in a tiny one-bedroom flat above an Indian restaurant in Tooting. I was still working as a cleaner for the Dabrowskis, but our relationship was becoming strained because they didn't approve of Antoni. They seemed to know he was a bad apple, but I just couldn't see it at the time. They terminated my contract after I was late for work on three separate occasions, and after that I was completely at Antoni's mercy, as I had no other way to support myself. No qualifications, no family over here, no savings. I had to rely on him to literally feed me and keep a roof over my head. That's when life began to get really bad...'

She paused again.

'Antoni is very manipulative, it's one of the ways he slithers through life like a snake, getting people to do his bidding,' Sylvie went on eventually. 'He can be very persuasive. Actually, the correct name for his behaviour – as I learnt later – is coercive. He told me that we would really struggle if I didn't help him earn some money. He said that if I didn't do as he said, then we wouldn't be able to be together, that there was no way he could support the two of us by himself. And that I'd have to return to my family in Poland in shame, and that they'd be so disappointed in me. So I felt that I had no other option. I had to do the things he demanded of me...'

A look of anguish flooded across Sylvie's face.

'What did he want you to do?' I said.

'Work as a prostitute from our flat.' Sylvie's voice was low now, her eyes half closed as she became lost in her memories. 'I was so ashamed, Polly. I had only had one other boyfriend – apart from Antoni – at that stage, I was still young and inexperienced. But he said there was no other option. So I just made myself get on with it...'

Her voice trailed off. I sat and waited, compassion rushing through me. *The poor woman. No wonder her face tells a story of hardship; she's certainly lived through some terrible times.*

'Antoni was so good at bringing me customers,' Sylvie went on. 'He seemed to know exactly what he was doing. And if I didn't earn what he wanted me to in a day, he would get furious. So angry. I can remember the first time that he hit me, it was when I was poorly. I'd had a bad cold that turned into bronchitis, but he wouldn't let me have any time off. Said I had to keep working. But I couldn't give the customers a good service, I felt too ill, all I wanted to do at the time was sleep. That night, after my lowest takings ever, he threw the money at me, then hit me round the face so hard that it made me fall to the floor.'

I was feeling so emotional now. I just wanted to reach across the table and give Sylvie a hug, tell her how sorry I was to hear what she'd been through.

'He apologised the next day, of course,' Sylvie said, her face grim. 'Said it had been my fault he'd been so angry because he was so worried about money, and I hadn't earned enough. Said he was sorry for losing his temper. But that started a pattern that just got worse and worse; he'd attack me when he wanted, then apologise the next day.'

'But why didn't you just leave him?' I said, the words coming out fast. My own relationship with Jakub had ended badly, but it had never been anything like this. 'Surely you could have found somewhere to go?'

Sylvie looked at me, then gave a weary smile.

'I don't know if you've ever been in an abusive relationship, Polly, but unfortunately it's not as easy as "just leaving",' she said. 'It's difficult to describe, but the abusive person somehow makes you completely co-dependent on them. Takes away all your independence, they even take away your mind. It's like all you have in your head is a confused fog. They've convinced you that you need them, that everything going wrong is actually your fault not theirs. That they are helping you in some way, and that you wouldn't survive without them. I know it's difficult to understand, but the power they've gained over you is immense. It was so difficult for me to leave Antoni, I wanted to for years. But it took me nearly losing my life to actually manage to do it...'

Chapter Four

'I'm thirty-six now,' Sylvie said. *Bless her*, I thought, *still a spring chicken compared to me, now I'm the ripe old age of forty-two*. 'And I was with Antoni until my late twenties, at which point he was charged with manslaughter and put into prison. I was pregnant with our son, Filip, when that happened. So after we reconnected, I was with Antoni for six long years before I managed to cut the ties. And most of that time was spent in a living hell.'

She sighed.

'There's not a day that goes by now where I don't thank God for my blessings,' she said. 'For finally being free from such a monster, and for giving me my angel child, Filip, who is a good friend of your nephew Oliver's by the way. For having this wonderful business, that seems to just get more and more successful every year. But my scars run deep, Polly. I can't even describe some of the awful things that Antoni made me do back then, they would be too graphic to put into the most explicit of books.'

'I'm so sorry, Sylvie,' I said, reaching out and grabbing one of her hands. 'What you've been through is just horrendous.

Antoni really does sound like a monster. I'm so glad he's locked away in prison now.'

Sylvie smiled and there was a warmth in her eyes when she looked at me. She squeezed my hand.

'Thank you,' she said. 'I have a feeling that we're going to work well together on this. But you haven't heard half of it yet. I still need to tell you what happened when things got really bad.'

Bloody hell, I thought. *How much worse can it get?* I realised that I hadn't even touched the delicious-looking sauerkraut that a smart young waiter had discreetly slipped onto the table while we'd been talking. I picked up my now lukewarm cappuccino and took a sip.

'One day I found a gun in Antoni's pocket,' Sylvie said. 'I was so angry, but by then it was difficult for me to show any emotion without him going mad. I asked him why he had it, and he said that he needed it for protection. That there were people who didn't like him and his friends. I never liked the people who came and hung out in our flat. They used drugs in front of me, the way they spoke was horrible. One of their girlfriends told me that Antoni was now quite high up in the Palace City Boys, which is a really bad gang from Crystal Palace. And that he was really respected; some of the younger members looked up to him as though he was almost a god. I was devastated, I couldn't believe that I'd got caught up in this type of life. I felt so trapped, Polly. It was unbearable.'

I nodded, it sounded like an awful way to live.

'After he got the gun, Antoni used it to terrorise me,' Sylvie said, tears making her eyes shine. 'He would put it up to my head and tell me to perform sex acts on him whenever he felt like it. He made me see more and more customers each week, and I was getting ill with all the stress. One day, I noticed that he had white flecks around his mouth, and I was immersed in that lifestyle enough by then to know that it meant he was smoking crack. His behaviour just got worse and worse, and I was constantly covered in bruises from when he'd batter me during his angry outbursts. The first time I got pregnant was when I was twenty-five. I knew that Antoni was the father because I always made sure that my customers used condoms, whereas me and Antoni never did. I was so happy, despite the shit state of my life. I was so looking forward to bringing a new life into the world, and I hoped that being a father would make Antoni calm down and change his ways. But one night...'

Sylvie stopped and took some deep breaths. Tears started rolling down her cheeks.

'One night,' she continued. 'When I was five months pregnant, Antoni and I were walking back towards our flat, when we were attacked by a group of at least seven men. I was thrown to the ground and stamped on repeatedly. I miscarried the next day.'

My hands went to my mouth.

'Oh, Sylvie,' I said. 'That's horrific, I'm so sorry you had to go through that.'

'Thanks, Polly,' she said, wiping her eyes. 'It was an awful time. It was after that that I decided I seriously needed to find a way out of all of this, otherwise I'd end up six feet under at some point. But I had to wait for the right time. That time found me in the end. I was finding more and more weapons in the flat; guns and all sorts of knives. I was living in constant fear, both of Antoni and of being attacked again. People we knew were being killed – they were all part of the Palace City Boys, and people who belonged to their main rivals, the Colliers Town Gang, were being murdered too. But no one would talk to the police, including me, so hardly anyone was ever charged. It was like living in hell. But a large part of Antoni was enjoying the notoriety, the infamy of being such a violent gangster.'

She paused, and took a sip of water.

'Antoni's drug use was getting worse and worse. He was smoking crack in front of me by that point, and took any other drug he could get his hands on. He started getting paranoid, thinking that I was working for the Colliers Town Gang in some way. He was always threatening me. Then one evening, after he was cracked off his head, he pushed me out of my car and shot at me – luckily he missed. Then he ran me over, breaking my left leg. He drove off, but this time I did go to the police. Things had gone too far, and I knew he'd end up killing me if I didn't do something to stop him. I was seven months pregnant with Filip at the time, who luckily was unscathed. To cut a long story short, Antoni was arrested a day later and I ended up testifying against him in court. He was given a fifteen-year sentence for attempted murder. I've hardly spoken to him since, just the odd time to update him about how Filip is doing. After all, he's Antoni's son too, even if he is a terrible father. But everyone deserves to know that their child is doing okay.'

She sat back in her chair, looking at me.

'Wow,' I said, exhaling. 'I mean, that is some story you've got there, Sylvie. I would be more than happy to help you turn it into a fantastic book.'

'Yes, that would be great, I'd like that,' Sylvie said. 'Thank you. I need to change my name, and also Antoni's and everyone else involved, because of the gang culture. These people are capable of terrible things, you know. And Antoni has high connections in the underworld. He's grandiose, or narcissistic if you want to call it that, to the point of being psychotic. He thinks he's so wonderful, such an esteemed gangster, that he once told me he thinks a statue of himself should be erected on his old patch. And I don't think he was joking. He wants to be forever immortalised somehow. And if anyone challenges his self-image, or tries to sprinkle a bit of truth on his delusions, then so help that person. He will go crazy. He probably hates me now, but I'm not going to let that stop me from telling my story. I'm done with letting him terrorise me. I just need to be careful, that's all. Be smart how I go about it, you know?'

'Yes,' I said. 'We can get legal advice about all that, Sylvie. And anyway, you don't need to worry about him anymore now, do you? He's locked away, so he won't be able to bother you any time soon.'

'Ah,' Sylvie said, shaking her head a little. 'Actually that's not entirely true, I'm afraid. I have it on good authority that Antoni has been behaving himself in prison recently. He's been inside for nearly nine years now, and has a parole hearing coming up. He might be released very soon, Polly. Not many inmates have to serve their entire sentences, especially if they've been toeing the line and keeping themselves out of trouble...'

Chapter Five

'So,' Marie said as she set a steaming mug of hot chocolate down in front of me. 'How did your meeting with Sylvie go? I want a blow-by-blow account. Every juicy detail.'

Sylvie and I had talked for ages that lunchtime, and we'd formerly agreed to go ahead with the ghostwriting project together. I'd explained to her that I always asked for a down payment of two hundred pounds at the beginning of a contract, as it showed a commitment from the client and cemented the deal. Sylvie had nodded and immediately reached into her apron, pulling out a wad of notes, almost as though she'd been ready for some sort of transaction like this. Perhaps Marie had given her a heads-up. She counted out ten twenty-pound notes, and pushed them across the table towards me.

'I'd like to start on this book as soon as possible,' she'd said. 'If that's okay with you, Polly?'

Of course it was okay! It was utterly fantastic, and it meant that I'd be able to start paying all my overdue bills, as well as get Danny some more exciting food as opposed to the cheap stuff we'd recently been eating. As a result – after I'd left Babka Eatery – I'd been walking on cloud nine for the rest of the afternoon. It didn't bother me that Antoni would perhaps be released from jail in the near future. Sylvie said that she no longer had anything to do with him, so I couldn't see that he'd pose any sort of problem. After all, he'd have the parole board watching him carefully if he was let out, and if he did anything stupid then he'd be recalled to prison. I watched quite a bit of true crime in the evenings, as those types of programmes provided rich material for my novels, which were so far self-published by me on Amazon. I'd dearly love to be signed by a 'proper' publisher, and hoped that this might just happen one day if I kept plugging away. And if I could just save up enough money to go on that creative writing course, well. Who knew what might happen...?

Yep, I thought. Antoni wouldn't cause me to lose any sleep, whether he was in or out of prison. I hoped that Sylvie wouldn't worry too much about him either. I liked her a lot, she was so dignified and together, especially given everything that that man had put her through. She'd shown me news reports about his sentencing on her phone at one point, and I'd seen Antoni's angry face staring back at the camera in the mugshot photo. He looked like a nasty piece of work. It was Sylvie's time to shine, she was ready to tell her amazing and heartbreaking story, and I was more than happy to be the one to help her do this. And anyway, perhaps Antoni was a reformed character now. Maybe he'd seen the error of his ways and would be ready to live a more positive, productive life whenever it was that he was freed...

Just before I was about to leave my house to pick Danny up from school, I'd received a text from my sister asking if we wanted to pop over to hers for a cuppa. I'd readily accepted. I liked nothing better than a chat with my sister, and for once I had a lot of news to tell *her*, instead of the other way around. It was turning out to be a good day.

'Well,' I said, cupping the hot mug in my hands as Marie sat down on the other side of the kitchen table. She was looking as glamorous as usual, in an expensive, stylish black top and mustard neck scarf. 'It all went very well. I'm hired. I officially have a new job! And I have you to thank really, Marie.'

She smiled.

'You know that I always find a way to look after my little sister,' she said with a wink. 'And it's an incredible story that Sylvie's got to tell, isn't it?'

'Shit, yeah,' I said. 'She's been through so much. Antoni sounds like a nasty piece of work. But if I'm honest, Marie, it's going to make a great book. And it's a project I can really get my teeth into. I don't mind writing elderly people's memoirs at all, but they can be a bit dry at times. A bit samey. Do you know what I mean?'

Marie nodded.

'Yep,' she said. 'Back in the good old days kind of stuff, when there was no technology and everyone went courting for years before they thought about getting married. No, Sylvie's book will be on a totally different level to that, Polly. Loads of sex and scandal to get your teeth into with that one. You won't have a moment to be bored when you're writing it.'

'Mmm,' I said, leaning back in my chair. I heard Danny shout then giggle in the playroom next door. He absolutely adored his older cousins, Bella and Oliver. I smiled, then looked over at my sister.

'Do you know Sylvie well then?'

'I mean, yeah I suppose so,' Marie said. 'We chat outside the school quite a lot. I find her really easy to talk to. Some of the other mothers there are alpha females who do yoga while baking cakes and simultaneously running their successful online businesses every day, and they can be quite hard work sometimes. Always want to talk about the kids' grades, and what healthy oat-based eating plan the whole family is on that month.

Whereas Sylvie is just normal, if you know what I mean. And she works very hard so that Filip can go to Aston Bennett. She wasn't born with a silver spoon in her mouth, unlike some of the yummy mummies there. I like her.'

'Me too,' I said, as Bella and Danny appeared at the kitchen door, both red-faced and panting. As I looked at Danny's cheeky blue eyes, his ruffled bright blond hair and how his face creased so adorably when he smiled up at me, my heart exploded with love as it always did when I looked at him. I felt so lucky and amazed to have produced – with the help of his dad, Jakub – such a precious and perfect little human being. 'What have you two been up to then?'

'Playing tag,' Danny said loudly. He'd definitely inherited the extrovert gene, I thought. Everything he did was confident and bold. Not a shy bone in his gorgeous little body. 'Can I have a drink please, Mummy?'

'Bella will get you one, won't you, darling?' Marie smiled at her nine-year-old daughter.

A couple of minutes later, Danny and Bella were back in the playroom, taking two large glasses of water and a plate of biscuits with them.

Marie's phone – lying next to her coffee mug on the table – bleeped into life. She stared at the number and her face went serious.

'Sorry, Poll, I have to take this,' she said as she picked up the device. She disappeared into the hall.

'Henry?' I could hear my sister saying in low tones. I hadn't intended to eavesdrop but Marie's always had a booming voice, even when she's trying to be quiet. 'What's the news?'

There was a pause.

'So they're not giving you the bonus?' she said, sounding strained. 'No, it's all right, calm down. We'll think of something.'

She must have walked further away at that point because

after that I could only hear murmurs. When she eventually came back into the kitchen, she looked different. No longer the carefree sister that I knew.

'Er,' I said, 'is everything all right? I wasn't listening or anything, but you look a bit stressed now, Marie.'

She looked at me, then sighed.

'Everything's okay really,' she said, running a hand through her hair. 'It's just that – for once – it's actually us having a few financial worries. Nothing too serious, and we'll be absolutely fine in the long run. The thing is, Henry had to remortgage the house last year as we still owed the builders a hefty sum for the last bit of the extension that they did. At the time, his income was blooming, so we thought that paying off a few thousand every month wouldn't be a problem.'

I tried not to gulp. *A few thousand a month? Blimey. My tiny mortgage was a few hundred a month, and that was hard enough for me to pay sometimes.* I'd got my little house with the inheritance our grandma had left to both of us, and I'm so glad I did. It was the wisest investment I'd ever made, and kept a roof over mine and Danny's heads when times got tough. But financial struggles were all relative, weren't they?

'Oh, Marie,' I said, suddenly feeling guilty that I couldn't help her out like she had with me in the past. 'I wish I could do something.'

My sister grimaced and waved a hand in the air.

'It's all fine really, Polly,' she said. 'Just means we have to tighten the straps for a few months, and be a bit more sensible with what is coming in. Don't you worry about it, we'll sort it. Now, back to Sylvie...'

We chatted on about my exciting new client for a while, and then Danny came in saying that he was absolutely starving.

'Time I got you home for some dinner then, isn't it?' I smiled at my blond-haired wonder boy. 'Shall we say thank you to Auntie Marie for having us over?'

During the drive home, I couldn't shake off my concerns about Marie and Henry. Money worries? Those two? It just didn't make sense. They'd always seemed so flush, so sorted financially. Hopefully Marie was right, and that whatever they were going through was just a blip and nothing to worry about. Because next to Danny, Marie meant everything to me, just like I did to her...

Chapter Six

Danny and I had a great evening together, we were both so happy – for different reasons. Danny was made up because he'd spent time with his beloved cousins; he adored them so much that he sometimes asked me if Bella and Oliver could be his brother and sister. He had the typical younger child hero worship of the older two, and I was so glad that his cousins were in his life because I could see that the older he got, the more he yearned for the rough and tumble playfulness that other children could provide. I wasn't planning on having any more children – which was probably wise as I didn't have a partner and wasn't looking for a new relationship any time soon. Therefore I was happy for Danny to spend as much time as possible with Bella and Oliver. And to gently explain to him – when he asked me to provide him with a brother or a sister – that this was unlikely to happen.

And I was personally ecstatic because the universe had thrown me a lifeline; I had a new ghostwriting client and I couldn't be happier with her. Sylvie had such an interesting – at times heartbreaking – story to tell, and I was so grateful for the fact that not only was she a nice person to work with, her book would be one that I really enjoyed writing. Meaty material that I could get my teeth into. And very different from the other books I'd written for people – which numbered nine to date. Don't get me wrong, I always enjoyed my work and appreciated my clients' stories and lives. They were all unique, and in their own way, all interesting. But Sylvie's tale was different, dark and dangerous. I'd never worked for a client who had a story that was touched by criminality and gangs. And I was strangely excited about getting started on this one...

The only thing slightly taking the shine off my mood was my concern for Marie and Henry: the Astors, Beckenham's golden couple. But I was less worried about them now than I had been at my sister's house.

Surely their money worries couldn't be that bad? I mused, as I found my favourite tune and turned it up as loud as I dared. 'Mississippi Goddam' by Nina Simone. Danny was soundly asleep upstairs and I didn't want to wake him up, he had school the next day and he was a boy who needed a good twelve solid hours. But it was a time for celebration. And I was pretty sure that Marie and Henry would sail through whatever financial issues they were having, unscathed. I mean, they had the cars, the enormous house, endless luxuries. How bad could things really be? No, I'd decided, I wasn't going to let my concerns for them spoil my new-found happiness. Christ, it was a welcome change from the permanent stress I'd been feeling recently, that constant tautness in my forehead that symbolised my daily worries about how we were going to eat and more generally survive. I felt quite giddy – euphoric even – because of the new job.

I didn't often drink, but I thought I might treat myself to a glass of red wine that evening. I went into the kitchen, and found a dusty bottle of Palataia Pinot Noir at the back of a cupboard and poured myself a nice, big glass. I'd always preferred red, I found white too vinegary. I took it into my tiny living room, sank back into the sofa and took a large sip as Nina Simone's husky tones filled the air.

I fired off a text to my friend, Brigitte, telling her all about my new job. She'd been more than aware of my money troubles, and had asked me only recently if I'd been able to find more work. Now I could tell her that I had!

My phone pinged a few minutes later.

Oh Polly, Brigitte had written back. *This is really marvellous news, I'm so pleased for you. Maybe you can write my life story for me one day?!*

Happy to, I replied. *I could come and stay in Roussillon with you for research purposes!*

Life is definitely on the up, I thought, putting my phone down again. A fizz of excitement came to life in my tummy. *Times are changing. I'm going to work so hard on this book, I want to make Sylvie happy and proud that she's chosen me as her writer. I think we are going to work well together. I can't foresee any problems at all at this stage. And I have my sister, Marie, to thank for facilitating this change in my circumstances. I must remember to buy her some chocolates and flowers...*

Chapter Seven

Sylvie's house was so clean and tidy, I thought as I looked around. I was sitting in her kitchen, and Sylvie was humming softly as she made us both a steaming mug of coffee. A framed photo of a thin, attractive blond boy wearing Aston Bennett's school uniform caught my eye – he must be her son, Filip. He looked like a sensitive, intelligent child. Her place was very unlike my own higgledy-piggledy one, which was more bohemian in style and clutter, and while I loved my décor it rarely looked like a show home. Whereas Sylvie and Filip lived in a nice new-build place on the edge of Beckenham; every room was painted white and had minimal new-looking furniture placed in it 'just so'. This was another contrast to my tiny old cottage, which had been standing for over two hundred years and was full of wonky walls, old beams, items and furniture that I'd collected from antique fairs over the years. 'Organised mess,' Marie called it. I preferred to think of it as strategic clutter.

'Right,' Sylvie said as she placed a mug in front of me, before sitting down. 'Where would you like to start, Polly?'

I clicked my Dictaphone on before I spoke; Sylvie had such a juicy story to tell that I didn't want to miss a word that she said about it. I'd emailed her the terms and conditions the evening before, and she'd readily agreed to everything and then asked when we could start. I was overjoyed at having such a dedicated and enthusiastic new client; and I had to admit that it was a big bonus that she could clearly afford the book and wasn't showing any signs of messing around with payments. I'd had a client before who would take weeks to pay me after I sent each instalment of words to them, and then would take several more weeks to pin down a date for the next interview. That sort of thing is infuriating when you're trying to earn your crust and pay your bills. But Sylvie was – so far – a dream to work with. And I was starting to really like her too. She was so self-sufficient; so on top of things, especially given everything she'd been through.

'Let's go back to the beginning,' I said, staring down at the Dictaphone to make sure it was working properly. It was. 'Why don't you tell me in more detail about your parents, your early childhood and what it was like growing up in Poland?'

So Sylvie did, giving good descriptions of her hard-working but strict father, Jan, and her indomitable mother, Agata, who worked hard to keep her five children in line – two boys and three girls – Sylvie being the middle child. Life had been tough for them, they'd had to save every penny and although they owned a café their parents sometimes didn't have a lot of food to give the children if takings hadn't been great. But they all got by, and were brought up with good morals and standards, always knowing right from wrong.

Unlike Antoni and his siblings, Sylvie said, who'd had a much worse start in life than her. His father had been a violent alcoholic who eventually left his wife for another woman, after terrorising her and their children for years. Left feeling a wreck and overwhelmed by life, Antoni's mother was unable to properly parent him and his siblings, and basically left them to run wild and bring themselves up. It was sad to watch, Sylvie said. The children all went downhill after that, wearing dirty clothes, being far too skinny, never being given haircuts. Everyone in the area felt sorry for them – especially when they were little. Some women tried to mother them, but Antoni and his siblings were too wild – feral – to be tamed properly for long. Then as Antoni grew up and showed signs of becoming a bad boy who thieved to get what he wanted, parents tried to keep their sons and daughters away from him.

'But I couldn't keep away,' she said, looking up at me. 'He just has such a strong magnetism to him, Polly. He can be so charming and persuasive, and make you feel like the most important person in the world, if he chooses to. Sometimes when I was with him, it felt like we were in our own little perfect bubble. I was infused with his energy, it was intoxicating. Do you understand what I mean?'

I nodded. I'd felt like that about Danny's dad, Jakub, at the start of our relationship, at least.

'But as you found out later he can also make you feel like the least important?' I said.

'Yes,' Sylvie said, nodding. 'That is very true. The flip side of Antoni is that he can be so cruel and selfish. He can also make you feel like you're the least, most insignificant person in the world. And I'm starting to think that I'll never be totally free from him, Polly.'

'What do you mean?' I said.

Sylvie paused for a minute, and when I looked up at her I was surprised to see that she was looking a little awkward.

'The thing is...' she went on, 'I had a call from the parole board yesterday evening when I got home from work. They told me that Antoni has been granted parole and needs a place in the community to be released into, somewhere safe where he can stay. He's not allowed to live in Beckenham anymore, as he can't be near me or Filip after everything he's done. And he can't be in or around Crystal Palace because of his gang connections. So they've found him a place in Dagenham. They asked me how I felt about it, and told me that parole officers and a social worker will be coming out to chat to me, and to give me advice on how best to avoid him, and what to do if he starts bothering us. He's going to live at this place in Dagenham just to start him off, until he can find somewhere more permanent to stay. I've had many visits from many different organisations since he ran me over, warning me about what he's capable of, so I'm used to this kind of thing. But it's crazy to think that he'll be out soon, and that I could bump into him at some point, even if I make an effort to avoid all the places where he's likely to go...'

'Wow,' I said, feeling my heart thumping at this news. 'Oh, Sylvie. How are you feeling about this?'

'Um...' Sylvie said. 'It's really strange, Polly. I've spent so much time being afraid of Antoni, hating him for what he did to me, and hoping he'd never get released. But listening to the parole officer, it sounds like he's really changed. Like he's been working on himself while he's been inside, you know?'

'Really?' I said. 'I mean, that sounds promising, and of course people can change their ways if they really want to. What did they say he was like now?' *Bloody hell*, I thought. *I hope Sylvie always remembers just how vile and dangerous Antoni was when he was with her. A changed man or not, he's someone she should always try and stay a million miles away from.*

'Well,' Sylvie said. She suddenly looked very different from the confident woman who I'd met the day before. Confused. Uncertain. 'They said that he'd worked hard to come off the drugs that he was addicted to when he came into prison, which I think was mainly crack. When he first got jailed he could be violent with the other inmates, and he got in trouble for that.

But apparently over the last few years he's been acting like a model prisoner, and even mentoring the newbies, helping them to settle in and calm down. Um...' She looked up at me. 'Antoni actually phoned me last night too, Polly. And it was such a surprise to hear his voice. I wasn't expecting to feel like I did at all, when I talked to him. He said such kind things, and he apologised over and over again for his past behaviour. He told me about how much he's changed as well, how he no longer takes drugs, how he's realised what is important in life, and how he just wants to get out and be normal. And how the parole board have realised this. He said he's missed me so much, and that he thinks about me every day and night. And he is Filip's dad, and he said he really wants to start to build a good relationship with his son...'

'Oh, right,' I said. I was feeling a bit shocked. This felt like a big turnaround from Sylvie's attitude yesterday, when she told me that she barely spoke to Antoni, and only did so on the odd occasion to update him about how Filip was doing. But hey, it was her life and it was really none of my business how she chose to run it. I was just the ghostwriter, there to observe and record. It was important that I kept my opinions to myself.

'The thing is,' Sylvie said, leaning forwards, 'that when I spoke to Antoni last night and heard him being so sweet, I realised just how lonely I've been lately, Polly. I've barely dated anyone since he went to jail, and it hasn't worked out with the few people who I have seen. There was just never the right chemistry there. And I kind of figured that the parole board must know what they're doing, they must have seen a big change in Antoni to let him out like this, don't you think? I mean, I'm not saying I want to see him or anything – please don't misunderstand me – but I think being on crack was the main thing that made him violent in the first place. And if he's off that, then he might have really pulled himself together and want to make a go of his life? I mean, sometimes people change, I mean *really* change, don't they? It just makes me feel a bit better about the idea that he'll soon be walking around on the streets near me and Filip...'

'Yeah,' I said. I didn't want to say too much, as I was feeling very conflicted about Sylvie's response and I was just her writer, after all. I didn't have any right to make judgements on her attitude or responses to things. But it was worrying me a bit that after a call from a parole officer and from Antoni himself, she could start easing off on her former approach, the one where she'd cut Antoni out of her life and had completely moved on from him. I really hoped that she didn't dwell on him being a changed man too much, as she might start seeing her former lover through rose-tinted glasses rather than the nice clear ones she'd been metaphorically wearing up till now. I didn't think that I'd feel the same as Sylvie; if someone had tried to kill me by running me over then I would probably hate them forever and not care if they'd changed for the better or not – I just would want them out of my life and head. But I didn't want to sound disapproving or judgy, as she was my new client – my only client – and I desperately needed this job to continue and be successful. And although I no longer got lonely being single, I did know what it felt like. In the months after Jakub and I had split up I'd often had a quiet cry in the evening, feeling like the only person in the world who wasn't spending their evening with a loved partner. Now I felt differently, I loved the freedom that being single gave me. But I knew where she was coming from all the same... 'Hopefully he has changed, Sylvie. Perhaps being locked up for so many years has had an impact on him and he wants to come out and live a better life. And if he wants to connect with his son again one day, I'm sure that there are people – maybe the social services – who can help you make that happen.'

We chatted on for another hour, with Sylvie going into more detail about her teenage years and her early relationship with Antoni. I nodded along, genuinely interested in everything she had to say. And her tales about what they used to do were as fascinating as they were shocking – the places Antoni broke into, the stuff he stole, how Sylvie protected him and hid his stolen loot.

But at the back of my mind, a little warning flag had sprung up. It had been there ever since she'd looked so hopeful when she'd told me that Antoni had changed his ways and now wanted a normal life. It had made me realise that there was going to be a lot more depth and complexity to me working with Sylvie than I initially realised. Because – to be honest – she was clearly not as sorted and decided about things as she'd first seemed. When I'd met her in the bistro that time, she'd seemed so together and strong, so keen on carrying on with her clean-living lifestyle. Then the minute she was told that Antoni had changed for the better, she'd got a wistful look in her eyes. She'd told me about feeling lonely, and it was a bit worrying that she'd made that connection after her former abuser had phoned her.

Maybe she'd never stopped being in love with him? I wondered. *Even though he'd done such terrible, unforgivable things to her? Perhaps she's spent all these years convincing herself that she's better off without him, but is questioning that now that Antoni sounds like he's improved his behaviour?* I'd never personally sought out dramatic people and a thrilling lifestyle, unlike my sister, Marie, who thrived on the drama that often reared its head within her group of friends. At school I'd been friends with the swots, as I genuinely loved working – saddo that I am. I liked peace and quiet. I was quite happy to drift through life, enjoying my quiet achievements – like taking on new writing jobs.

A thought struck me. *How would Antoni react if he ever*

found out that Sylvie was writing this book? One that detailed her life with him in a 'warts and all' kind of way? She'd been scared of him and his associates finding out about that, hadn't she? Wanted to change her name so that word didn't get out about what she was doing? Then another thought struck me. *If Antoni ever did find out about the book, Sylvie may well cancel the project.* I knew this was a selfish way to think and I berated myself for it, especially when Sylvie had been through so much and was being so brave by telling the world about her experiences. But I couldn't help desperately hoping that Antoni wouldn't find out about what she was doing, and that the project would continue unimpeded. I'd just begun to let myself believe that Danny and I might be okay financially soon, and that I could even begin saving up for the creative writing course...

I needed this job so badly, I couldn't bear to think of losing it so soon after getting to know her and being so gobsmacked by her life story. And – as a consequence – finally believing that I would actually be able to pay my bills for the next few months... *Maybe I should find a way to gently remind my new client about how important it was that Antoni never got word about this ghostwriting project?*

Chapter Eight

It was two days since my interview with Sylvie, and I was immersed in writing up the initial part of what she'd told me. I'd got quite a bit done in the daytime, but then Danny had come home from school a bit grumpy as he'd had a falling out with his best friend, Toby, about some playground football game or other, and it had taken him ages to finally settle and go to bed, convincing him that he and Toby were bound to be best buds again the next day, once they'd both had a good rest.

Every time I sat down at the kitchen table, laptop in front of me, I'd hear my son's little footsteps padding down the stairs.

'Mummy, I can't sleep. I've had a nightmare.'

'Danny, you can't have had a nightmare, as you haven't even been to sleep yet. You just need to relax, darling. Go on, off you go back to bed.'

Ten minutes later...

'Mummy, I'm really thirsty. Can I have a drink?'

'Yes of course, darling. Hang on a second...'

Christ, I'm never going to get any work done at this rate, I thought, sending my son – who knew all the distraction techniques ever invented – back to bed for the umpteenth time.

Then finally, from the ongoing quietness upstairs, it seemed that Danny must have fallen asleep at last.

Brilliant, I thought, checking the time on my phone. *It's only half nine, I've got a good few hours to work on Sylvie's book now.*

Then my phone bleeped into life. *Fucking hell*, I thought, grabbing it in frustration. Then I did a double take at the name flashing up. It was Oliver, Marie's son. Both her children had been given phones practically as soon as they could talk – apparently this was normal for pupils in Aston Bennett – and she'd listed my number in both my niece and nephew's devices, in case of emergency.

'Hi,' I said, answering the call. 'Oliver, is that you?'

'Yes, Auntie Polly, it's me,' my nephew said. 'Do you know where Mum is?'

'What?' I said. 'Surely she's at home with you, Oliver?'

'No, she's not here and neither is Dad,' he said. 'I was upstairs on the PlayStation, and I just came down to say goodnight to Mum but I can't find her anywhere. Bella's already asleep. I know where Dad is, he had to work late tonight. But Mum was supposed to be here with us.'

'Oh,' I said, confusion coming over me. 'Have you tried calling her?'

'Yes,' Oliver said. 'But she's not answering.'

'Hmm,' I said, thinking fast. This was odd. Something that had never happened before. I didn't want to worry him, but at the same time I couldn't think where Marie would be. *Maybe she's popped round to a neighbour's for a minute, or something. Perhaps she'd really wanted a cup of tea only to find that there wasn't any milk in the fridge.* 'I tell you what, let me try and call her. I'll phone you back very soon. Okay?'

'All right,' Oliver said. He didn't sound very happy.

I rang off and tapped on Marie's number straight away. But all I heard was the ringing tone going on for ages.

Shit, I thought. Danny was finally asleep and I didn't want to wake him up and drag him over to his cousin's house unless it was absolutely necessary. I'd never get him back to sleep after that and he'd be in a foul mood in the morning. Obviously I would if I couldn't get hold of my sister, but it would be much easier if she just answered her bloody phone... I tried Marie's number again. Then again.

'Polly?' She answered it on the third try. 'You okay?' She sounded breathless.

'Yes I'm fine,' I said. 'Marie, where are you? Oliver's just phoned me – he says you're not in the house with him and Bella? He was looking for you as he wanted to say goodnight before he went to bed.'

'Oh crap,' Marie said. It sounded like she was getting into her car or something, I could hear keys jangling in the background. 'I just popped out for some bread as the kids always eat toast in the morning and I realised that we've run out. I forgot that Oliver was still up actually. Thought he'd already gone to bed. I'll be back there in five minutes, but I'll phone him now, Poll, and reassure him. Thanks, babes.'

She rang off.

How weird, I mused, lying my phone back on the kitchen table. *How can you forget that your child is not in bed? Ah well*, I thought – immediately forgiving, *Marie has a lot more going on in her life than I do. And two children rather than one. She probably just had a senior moment, must have had a busy day.*

Now... I turned my attention back to my screen. It was time for some serious writing. If I didn't get any more interruptions...

Chapter Nine

'Hi, Sylvie?' I said. 'Are you free to chat for a minute or two?'

'Polly,' Sylvie said in her lilting accent. 'Great to hear from you. Is everything okay with the book?'

'Oh yes,' I said. 'It's fine, I've made a great start on it. You have such a powerful story to tell, Sylvie, and I want to make sure that I get it just right for you. I'm still working through the material from the interview we've just done, and there are a couple of follow-up questions I have actually, if that's all right?'

'Sure,' she said. 'Fire away.'

So I asked her for clarification about a few points to do with her childhood, like how many bedrooms there had been in her parents' house, who had shared with who, and what it had been like living in such close quarters with her siblings. I asked if it would be okay if I turned my Dictaphone on again and recorded her answers, which she readily agreed to. It was so important that I did justice to Sylvie's story, I really wanted her tale of surviving adversity to be as magnificent as possible. Sylvie answered my questions fully, adding to the already fantastic material I had from her.

'Just one more thing,' I said when she'd finished explaining. 'Ah, a thought crossed my mind, Sylvie, after the last time we chatted and you told me that Antoni would soon be getting out of prison. I know that when we talked in your bistro, you asked me to make sure that I keep all of this information confidential, which of course, I will. You've told Marie a lot of your story, but I will never tell anyone else. Presumably this is because you don't want Antoni or any of his gang associates to find out that you're writing this book?'

Sylvie sighed down the phone.

'Exactly, Polly,' she said. 'This thought has been bothering me too. I feel so strongly about telling my story; I want to be able to inspire other women who might be going through similar abusive situations, and to let them know that there is light at the end of the tunnel. That they can survive, and not only that, that they can get away from their abuser and live a good life, and be happy and successful. In order to do this, I have to write it under an assumed name of course, but the truth of what I have been through will be out there. If Antoni finds out about it then of course he will try and stop me; he is proud and arrogant, and however much he's changed for the better, I know that he won't want me telling the world about the bad things that he's done in the past. But it's not only him that I'm worried about; if I'm going to be honest then I have to be able to tell you about what his gang – the Palace City Boys – got up to. We can change their gang name in the book of course. They – and him – were involved with criminal activity on every level, and this impacted my life in various ways. So don't worry, I am going to do everything I can to keep this book under wraps so that we can carry on with it without anyone causing us trouble. I feel like it's my life's work in a way, although that might sound funny to you. It's my voice, my ultimate freedom from abuse, to be able to share what I've gone through and overcome with the world.'

'It doesn't sound strange at all,' I said, suddenly feeling quite emotional. 'It makes perfect sense, Sylvie. And I want so much to be able to help you do that. You're literally the bravest person I've ever met; to have been treated like that by Antoni and then to heal and grow into the successful businesswoman that you are today, you really are an inspiration.'

'Thank you, Polly,' Sylvie said. 'I'm so thrilled that Marie put us in touch with each other, and that you're the one writing my book for me. I have a feeling that you're going to do a magnificent job of telling my story.'

'Well, I hope so,' I said. 'I'm going to do my utmost with it, Sylvie. Okay, that's fab. Thank you for answering my extra questions, and there's no reason at all why Antoni would ever find out about this book. We'll have it written before you know it, and then like you say, the world will know what you've been through and how you've since thrived, and I'm sure that many women will be inspired because of what they read about you.'

We said our goodbyes, and rang off. As I sank into the sofa, a strange and wonderful sensation came over me. I was suddenly feeling a bit wet around the eyes. I'd never felt like I'd done anything that useful in the world before – not anything out of the ordinary, I mean. Having said that, Danny was beyond extraordinary, and every day I regarded him as the most perfect work of art ever created. But I'd never achieved anything in a humanitarian sense before; been in the position to help the world, do a greater good kind of thing. But the realisation had just come over me that by writing this book for Sylvie, I could do a small piece of that. By helping her to tell her story, I would be helping to get her voice out into the public sphere. The voice of an abuse survivor, a very brave woman, who had faced such terrible odds, yet overcome them and had built a successful business up. Like a phoenix rising from the ashes. *Yes*, I thought. *It made me feel good to be a part of this*. I was no longer just writing the book in order to earn money, I was now emotionally invested in the project too. It would be my small way of doing something useful for once, and helping to shine a light on the incredible way that Sylvie had overcome such terrible abuse and adversity. I felt proud to be working with her.

I stood up, wiped my eyes, and went and sat back in front of my laptop...

Chapter Ten

I pushed the bistro door open. Sylvie, who was by the till, looked up and waved.

'Come and sit down, Polly,' she called. 'I've saved us the same table as before.'

I'd had so much great material on my Dictaphone from our last chat, that I'd spent the last ten days writing it up and forming the beginning part of her book. It was important to set the scene, to anchor the person in a place, space and time, in order for the reader to connect well with them. I desperately needed to get this bit right, and for my client to be pleased with it. And I was doubly invested now; that feeling of doing something useful for once had stayed with me, and I was anxious to do justice to Sylvie's story, to portray her life exactly as she'd described it to me, so that the reader would feel like they were living through her experiences with her. A couple of days ago I'd nervously emailed off six thousand words to Sylvie – a double instalment of my usual three thousand words, and then hardly slept that night – worrying that she'd hate what I'd written and text me to say that our arrangement was off. But when I came back from dropping Danny at school the next day, a message pinged into life on my phone. It was from Sylvie asking for my bank details so that she could transfer me the payment for the writing. I was so overjoyed when I saw her message that tears actually sprang to my eyes. I could pay off the water bill, the gas bill and some of the electricity one too. And I'd even be able to help Marie out a little bit if she got into dire straits.

A few minutes after I'd texted her back with my bank info, another message popped up from Sylvie telling me that she'd transferred the money, and asked if I'd like to come over to her bistro again the following day for the next interview.

I walked over and sat down, with a well-prepped waiter immediately placing a coffee and a plate of delicious-looking biscuits in front of me. Sylvie slid into the chair opposite me a few moments later, I turned my Dictaphone on and we soon became immersed in the next section of her life. Sylvie described to me – in great detail – the bigger crimes that Antoni began to commit during their teenage years in Poland. How he'd steal cars, then take her on long joyrides. How her parents began to despair of their wayward daughter, imposing stricter and harsher punishments on her, and how, for a while at least, she found ways to get around these, like climbing out of her bedroom window at night when everyone else was asleep.

'I really was a wild child back then,' Sylvie said, a grin coming over her face as she reminisced. 'Of course, I'd hate it if Filip behaved like that when he's a bit older, but it was a lot of fun, Polly. Until it wasn't. Do you know what I mean?'

I smiled back at her and nodded. I was the square one in the family; it had been my sister, Marie, who'd behaved more like Sylvie and rebelled in her teenage years. I remembered the time when my sister said she was going to a friend's house to do homework one Friday evening when she was about seventeen, but had actually got the train into Charing Cross with a group of friends and gone clubbing all night. My parents had been livid when she'd finally got home the next morning, bleary eyed and exhausted, more because she'd lied to them rather than anything else. I'd stayed in my room that Saturday, my head in a book, listening to Dad tear strips off Marie, telling her she was grounded indefinitely from that moment on, with my sister screaming back at him, telling him that he didn't understand her and that he couldn't treat her like a baby forever. I couldn't help wondering what Danny would be like when he got older. He was much more outgoing than I'd ever been, much more at ease with making friends. Maybe he would have some of the liveliness I'd lost; I kind of hoped he would. I should probably be prepared for a bit of rebelling from him at some point. *But that's years away,* I thought contentedly. *He's still into dinosaurs and teddy bears at the moment. And thank goodness for that.*

'But then one day I found an earring in his latest nicked car,' Sylvie said, a look of pain flitting across her face. 'And I knew straight away that it wasn't mine. I only wore studs, but this was a big loopy one. I asked Antoni who it belonged to, and he gave me some vague story about giving his sister a lift somewhere. But something didn't seem right to me about it. He barely talked to his sister at that stage, so the idea of him actually giving her a lift was far-fetched. And where would she need to go? She was a street kid like him. She just hung around in Gruszki village.'

She went on to tell me about more signs she'd found, red flags that suggested that Antoni was seeing another girl behind her back.

'People started telling me things,' she said, looking sad. 'For a while I ignored them, I didn't want to face the truth. I really did love Antoni then. He had such a big hold over me, and although I was so young I just couldn't imagine my life without him, you know?'

I nodded. Now that was something I could definitely relate to. It's how I'd felt about Danny's dad, Jakub, for many years.

'But Antoni was becoming less subtle with his behaviour,' Sylvie went on. 'And one night, I saw him and this other girl, Kalina, coming out of a bar together. And I just knew...'

She paused, and I was surprised to see such a large amount of pain in her eyes. *Oh dear*, I thought. *From the looks of things, I don't think Sylvie has ever truly stopped loving this monster, Antoni. Bless her. Well, I know from experience how hard it can be to cut ties with a person you love, even if their behaviour towards you has become destructive.* Then a thought crossed my mind...

'Er, Sylvie,' I said. 'Any update about Antoni being released from jail?'

'Yes,' she said, her eyes snapping up to meet mine. 'He's already out, Polly.'

Then the strangest look flashed across her face. At first I couldn't read it. What was it? Guilt? Defensiveness?

'And have you heard from him at all?' I said instinctively.

'Y-yes,' she said slowly, as though deciding whether or not to divulge this particular bit of information to me. 'He rang me two days ago. Wanted to let me know that he's out and he's doing okay. And he wanted to know how Filip is.'

The next question I wanted to ask – that was on the tip of my tongue – was: *And have you actually seen him?* But I couldn't say it, it was none of my business. I was just the ghostwriter. And I had to trust Sylvie's choices. She was an amazing woman, she'd been through so much. And she knew what getting back in touch with Antoni would mean; what was at stake. Not just the book she was writing, but her actual safety. And that of her son's. But I was getting the feeling – more and more – that the amazing woman sitting opposite me had never fully stopped loving Antoni. And as I knew from experience, love could make the most rational people do the most inadvisable things.

I just nodded, and kept silent. Sylvie chatted on a bit more about her teenage break-up, but I couldn't stop wondering about whether she'd seen Antoni. Because if she had, it would mean that she'd met up with him almost as soon as he'd got out of jail. And she was in such a good place now, with her life, her son and her business. Not to mention her security and safety. I realised that I'd begun to see her as more than just a client; I really liked her. I'd begun to regard her as a friend too. And the thought of her jeopardising everything she'd built up for an awful man who didn't deserve another moment of her time gave me the chills...

Chapter Eleven

Two weeks later, I was walking down the pavement towards Sylvie's house feeling a tad apprehensive. A lot had happened in her life since I'd last seen her in her bistro; we'd kept in constant telephone contact, and it had gradually become clear that – at least to some extent – Antoni was wheedling his way back into her life. And I could tell, from her excited tones when I chatted to her, that she was not exactly dismayed by this. It was as though she'd somehow drawn a line under the past, put to bed the fact that he'd tried to kill her, and was blindly absorbed in her belief that he was a changed man.

Sylvie had been reluctant to tell me about her contact with Antoni at first, but my sixth sense had sussed it out, and I'd asked a few questions. She'd slowly opened up, and one day had revealed to me that the two of them had actually met up in a park.

'He's back to being his old self, Polly,' she'd said. 'He's totally off the drugs, and in fact he writes to the men he made friends with in prison, encouraging them to stay clean. It's amazing. He's like the Antoni I first got to know back in Poland. Before he started doing the bad stuff. I really do believe that prison has been good for him. You know?'

'Wow,' I'd said. 'That's amazing, Sylvie. I'm so pleased.'

Trust her, I kept telling myself. *She's an intelligent woman who loves her son to death. She'd never do anything to put Filip in harm's way*. But the doubts at the back of my mind wouldn't disappear. *Why is she doing this?* I wondered. *She has a chance to live an Antoni-free life now. Why is she rekindling contact with him? Because she still loves him*, I answered. *It's obvious. And love isn't sensible, is it?*

Then a few days later, she dropped a bombshell.

'Antoni and I went out for a drink last night,' Sylvie said. 'Marie came round to babysit Filip for me.' Blimey, I thought, grinning to myself. My sister rarely even does that for me. She must really like Sylvie. 'And I ended up telling Antoni about the book you and I are writing together.'

I almost dropped my phone. *You did what?* I thought. *Are you joking here, Sylvie? After everything we talked about? Say something, Polly. Ask her what the hell she is playing at...*

'Oh,' I said, feeling my throat get tighter. 'And, ah, what did he say?'

'Oh, Polly,' Sylvie said. 'He was so supportive. He thinks it's a really great idea. Don't worry, I wouldn't have said a word about our project to him unless I was absolutely sure he'd take it well. But he really is a changed man. It's amazing. Prison has been so good for him. He listens to me now, he's much more compassionate. And he genuinely wants to lead a better life. A normal one. And he's so sorry for the things he's done in the past. For being in that gang, his criminal activity and for hurting me. I've never seen such a change in a person before. Antoni actually said that he wants me to be honest, he wants me to tell you everything that he's done, so he can be held up as an example to other young gang members, showing them what happens when you do wrong. That he got sent to prison to learn the error of his ways.'

'Blimey,' I said, my head reeling. 'Wow. That's great, Sylvie.' I could feel my doubts about Antoni begin to lift at that moment. It really did sound like he'd changed. Like he'd become a bigger, better person than the danger to society that he'd been before. 'I'm so glad that he wants to collaborate with you on this.'

'With *us*, Polly,' Sylvie said. 'He wants to work with you as well as me. I told him all about you, and what an amazing writer you are. How you understand me, and what I've been through. And he really wants to meet you.'

'Oh,' I said. 'Does he?'

And that, I thought, *was the exact conversation that led to me walking towards Sylvie's house now*. Two days ago Sylvie had rung me to tell me to arrange a day when I could come over to her house and meet Antoni.

'The parole people said that he shouldn't come to my house,' she'd said. 'Because of our son. But they know he's changed and if only they could understand exactly who Antoni is now – like I do – and how he's bettered himself, I'm sure they wouldn't mind. He's been to see me twice now, both times when Filip was at school. I know this was against the orders as it was at my house, but it's really fine now. He's so different, Polly. He apologised to me for everything and said he regrets behaving like he did.'

Right, Polly, I told myself as I walked up to her door. *There's no need to feel nervous; Antoni's a changed man and he could be a real asset to this book. The money you're earning is great, and the best thing is that you're giving Sylvie – and now Antoni – a voice. The end product could be even more powerful with his input; a warning to young gangsters as well as an inspirational book for abuse survivors.*

I rang the doorbell.

'Oh hi, Polly,' Sylvie said, as she opened the door. 'Come in. It's so nice to see you again.'

As soon as I saw her, the butterflies in my stomach began to disappear. Because she looked so genuinely happy, and much more at ease than she'd ever seemed before. Glowing, in fact. I followed her down the squeaky clean little hall and into her living room, where a muscly-looking man was sitting on the sofa. *Blimey*, I thought, taken aback. I hadn't been expecting Antoni to be quite so attractive. So much better-looking than the angry man I'd seen in the mugshot photo that Sylvie had shown me on her phone when we were in the bistro the first time. And I hadn't thought he would have quite such a ravishing smile.

'Polly?' the man said, standing up and holding out his hand. 'It's so nice to meet you. Sylvie has told me all about you. I think it's fantastic that you are writing her book for her.'

I stuck out my hand and shook his, trying to take in every detail about him. His accent was thicker than Sylvie's, but his English was pretty excellent. His arms – or what I could see of them – were covered in tattoos, his brown hair closely cropped. His eyes were sharp, and I felt like he was taking everything in about me, as much as I was with him. His red lips were still smiling – he did have a great smile. I was starting to understand why Sylvie was still clearly attracted to this man. He had a presence, he exuded confidence.

'Please,' Antoni gestured towards an armchair, 'sit down, Polly. I want to get something out of the way before you guys start, if it's okay with you. The elephant in the room, as they say. I know you've heard pretty terrible things about what I was like in the past, and I just want to tell you that they are all true, and that I am one hundred per cent sorry for everything I've done. I was a bad man, back then. I don't want to make excuses for my behaviour as I take responsibility for that – the classes in prison helped with this – but I have to admit that when I started smoking crack all those years ago, it changed me. I was off my head for a while and poor Sylvie got the worst of it. If I could turn back the clock and do things differently, then I would. But I can't. The best thing I can do, is to work with you guys on this book, if you'll let me? I want to help Sylvie tell her story. She's an amazing human being. And I want to warn other young idiots who are like I was then; tell them to stay out of trouble. Off the drugs. Show them what might happen if they don't. Does all this make sense?'

I nodded, feeling taken aback. I hadn't expected him to be quite so brutally honest so quickly.

'Er, yes,' I said. 'It sounds great, Antoni. I'm so proud to be working on this book with Sylvie, because as you just said, she's an amazing woman, with a really powerful story to tell. And it sounds like your input could help make the project even better.'

Antoni smiled.

'Fantastic,' he said. 'I'd like to stay in the room and listen to Sylvie talk, if that's all right with you? See which bit you guys have got up to? I promise I'll keep quiet and not interrupt.' He flashed his white teeth at me again.

'Yes,' I said, taking my bag off my shoulder and sitting down. 'That's fine with me.' I was feeling a lot more relaxed now, after meeting Antoni in person. I could see what Sylvie meant when she'd described his charisma. He seemed like a genuinely nice person. In fact, it was hard to imagine him doing anything awful. But then, as he'd said, the drugs had changed him back then. Turned him into a different person, and made him make bad choices. *He looks very healthy now*, I thought, glancing over at him. *And he's clearly willing to be honest and support this book. Bit of a surprising turn of events, having Antoni being a part of it all, but hey, it could just turn out to be for the best...*

I retrieved my Dictaphone and turned it on. A brief thought

flashed across my mind about how much of a sheltered life I'd led compared to some people. Antoni and Sylvie were so worldly, they'd been through good and bad extreme experiences. Whereas I'd been plodding along pretty normally really. Working hard, not bothered that I had a small group of – very good – friends, not going out much. Granted, splitting up with Jakub had been awful – funnily enough he also had Polish parents but had been born and bred in South London – but no more hideous than normal break-ups. He'd never attacked me, taken drugs, made me be a prostitute or run me over. I looked up at Antoni. Whereas this man had done all those things to Sylvie. *How could someone do all that to another person?* Suddenly the butterflies in my stomach were flittering back...

Sylvie came in expertly balancing three coffees on a tray, and it wasn't long before we were up and running with the next interview. We'd already covered everything up to the point where Antoni had cheated on her when they were teens back in Poland, so I suggested that she pick up the story from that point on.

'I'd already left school by then,' Sylvie said, grinning over at Antoni, who winked back at her. *Crikey,* I thought. *Is there more than just a working relationship going on with them now? So soon? It's none of your business, Polly,* I told myself immediately. *Just concentrate on what she's saying.* 'I was working in my mum and dad's café in Gruszki village. It was a pretty basic establishment, but it was usually busy as a lot of the locals came there to get breakfast or lunch. I was slowly regaining my parents' trust. They'd nearly disowned me when I was running the streets with Antoni, my dad told me that I'd brought disgrace on the family, as before that they were well thought of in Gruszki. I'd managed to hide a lot of what had gone on from them, but they weren't stupid, and other people in the village told them things about Antoni and I. But after we'd broken up I wanted to prove to my parents that I was a good girl who they could trust.' She broke off and smiled shyly at Antoni. He raised an eyebrow in return. 'My parents had always favoured my older sister, Morela, and I used to be very hurt by this. I was really jealous of how they doted on her and thought she could do no wrong. But then I realised that she'd never done what I had, Morela had never sneaked out of the house to smoke pot with boys, or hidden stolen goods in her bedroom. I realised that my parents had a reason for praising her so much. And I wanted to make them as proud of me as they were of her.'

I nodded.

'By the time we got the call from the Dabrowskis – the family who'd come to England and set up the cleaning business – my relationship with my parents and siblings was much better than it had been for a long time,' Sylvie said. Then she stopped talking and a look of deep sadness overtook her face. 'My mother is dead now,' she said. 'And I miss her. She had breast cancer, and it spread really fast. In the end, there wasn't anything that the doctors could do to help her. I regret not getting to know her better while I had the chance. She was always so busy, and for a while I disrespected both her and my father. But I'm glad that things got better between us before I moved to England.'

I nodded again, and waited for her to continue.

'I was very excited about travelling to this country,' Sylvie said. 'My parents trusted the Dabrowskis and knew that they were good people, so they were happy to let me go. They said that if I could send back some of my earnings to them then they would really appreciate that. So I did, for as long as I had the cleaning job anyway. And I was pleased to be able to help them out for once. And when I started doing the, er, escorting work, I continued to send back what I could to them, although it wasn't nearly as much at that point.'

'Sorry, Sylvie,' Antoni said, leaning forwards. 'Do you mind if I just interrupt for a second? You might have forgotten but you were paid very well for the escorting and massage work that you did. I just wanted to remind you, as you were making it sound like you weren't.'

Sylvie nodded immediately and gave him another grin. He gave her another wink and patted her hand.

'Yes,' she said. 'Yes, you're right, Antoni. You always gave me some money for that, didn't you?'

Hmm, I thought. *He just corrected her. It was a small thing, and he'd been very polite about it, but the correction had been there nevertheless. And she'd immediately – almost unconsciously – submitted to his reasoning.*

When I'd chatted to Sylvie the first time in the bistro, she'd said that when Antoni forced her to become a prostitute she'd been entirely dependent on him. So did he really give her money to spend and send back to her parents? *Maybe you got it wrong the first time, Polly,* I thought, glancing at Antoni, who was now listening intently to Sylvie as she carried on talking. *Maybe you got the wrong end of the stick and Sylvie had meant to just say that there was a difference in her earnings. He's a changed man now, you can see that. Don't worry about such a small thing.*

The rest of the hour passed fairly quickly, with Sylvie telling me in detail about how she'd felt when she'd arrived in England, what it had been like living with the Dabrowskis – 'They were nice but even more Catholic than my parents' – and how she'd started feeling lonely as she worked away as a cleaner, yearning to have more contact with her own age group. Wondering if she'd ever date anyone again. She was obviously more of a people person than me, needed others to be around her for her to be happy. Whereas I was just fine with it being me and Danny. Antoni had chipped in here and there, reminding her of a couple of names she'd forgotten, agreeing with her about what life was like in Gruszki village. It was nice to see them working together in harmony, and this reassured me about his earlier interruption.

After I'd said my goodbyes, promising Sylvie that I'd write up the next instalment as soon as I could, I drove back to my house feeling thoughtful. So people really can change, I mused. Antoni still had a presence – a powerful air – about him, but he was clearly no longer the monster that had run Sylvie over all those years ago. He'd seemed enthusiastic, like he genuinely wanted to help her with her book writing. *Maybe this really will work out for the best,* I thought. *The three of us bringing Sylvie's amazing story to life...* As I turned a corner, I wondered what my sister made of the whole thing. After all, Sylvie had said that Marie had babysat for her when she'd gone out for a drink with Antoni that night, so I wouldn't be breaking any confidentiality agreement by mentioning that I'd also met him. Getting to know Sylvie had been such a momentous event in my life, that it was nice that I had at least one other person I could chat with about it all. *Maybe I should give Marie a ring,* I thought. *Suggest we meet up. She's been strangely silent recently, usually she's texting me about hilarious PTA dramas and stuff. I should probably check that everything's okay with her and Henry, and that things are getting better with their financial worries...*

Chapter Twelve

'Babe,' Marie's voice was saying down the phone. I smiled. She usually only called me babe when she wanted something. 'Babe,' she said again. 'You couldn't be an absolute lifesaver and have Bella to sleep over at yours tonight, could you? Henry's only just told me that there's an important work dinner thing we have to go to tonight – it's a bring-your-partner-along one – and I'm trying to find last-minute childcare for the kids. I actually thought it was only him who had to go to it, but he's told me at the last minute – obviously – that he needs me to be there too. Oliver's going to stay the night at a friend's house, but Bella's bestie has the flu.'

'Yes of course,' I said, beginning to unpack my bag of hastily purchased groceries with one hand. 'Danny absolutely loves Bella, I'm sure he'd be thrilled to have her here for a sleepover.'

'Oh God, thank you, Poll, you're an absolute star.' My sister's voice was getting louder, like it always did when she was relieved or excited. 'I'll drop her off to you at about six. Is that all right?'

'Yes, yes, that's fine,' I said. 'Actually, Marie, I was wondering if you wanted to meet up for a chat and a coffee soon? Things are going really well with Sylvie and the book, and there have been some developments...'

'Oh that's great, Poll,' Marie said. 'Yeah, she was telling me all about what a changed man Antoni is when I was having drinks with her the other night. Listen, I'd love to have a good chat with you about this now, but I literally have five minutes in the high street before I have to go and pick up the kids from school. I have to quickly find something to wear for the dinner this evening, because none of my other dresses fit well anymore. I've clearly eaten too many PTA cakes. But then, I've never been as skinny as you, have I, Poll?'

'Oh,' I said. 'No, that's absolutely fine, Marie. We can always get together another time. You carry on with your shopping, and I'll see you and Bella at about six this evening.'

We said our goodbyes, and I put the phone on the sideboard. As I was unpacking the rest of the groceries, I wondered what it must be like having a husband who whisked you off to glamorous work dinners without a moment's notice. *Wonderful if you like that sort of thing*, I decided. *Personally, I'd rather be curled up on the sofa under a blanket, tapping away on my laptop or reading a good book.*

Then another thought struck me: *Had Marie just said that she'd been having drinks with Sylvie?* I blinked. It had struck me as a bit strange, because before – when we'd chatted – she'd indicated that she only knew Sylvie as a playground mum. But obviously they were a bit closer than that, if they'd been out drinking together, and Marie had babysat Filip. Not that there was anything wrong with them being good friends at all, Marie had always been the most social one out of the two of us. I just didn't know they were so close, that was all. But it really wasn't a big deal. *Now*, I thought, stuffing a bag of frozen peas into the freezer. *What should I give the kids for dinner later?*

The sound of screeching tyres outside at five to six that evening signalled the arrival of my sister and niece. Within seconds, I could hear the two of them arriving at the front door – both talking loudly as always.

'Hi,' I said with a grin, as I opened the front door. 'Come in. Danny is so excited to have you here for a sleepover, Bella.' Behind them, the early evening sky was already pretty dark.

'Hello, Auntie Polly,' Bella said as she bounced in, her russet hair tumbling over her shoulders. 'I've brought three board games with me. Where's Danny?'

'He's in the living room, sweetheart,' I said. And with that, she was off to find her cousin.

I turned my attention to my sister, and hesitated for a moment as I took in the outfit she was wearing. *Crikey,* I thought. *This is not the kind of stuff you usually wear, sis.* Marie and all of her very voluptuous figure was stuffed into a bright red – very short – bodycon dress that didn't leave much to the imagination. I was used to my sister looking glamorous in elegant, sweeping, black dresses and dripping in diamonds and pearls when she went out. So this was a bit of a big change in attire, and it looked like she was wearing the kind of jewellery I'd buy from H & M, rather than her usual classy stuff. Which wasn't a problem, it was just unexpected and different.

'Wow,' I said, trying to find the right words. 'You look very, er, fashionable.'

'Is it too young for me?' Marie said, sounding rather uncertain. She smoothed the sides of the dress down with her hands. 'I hardly had any time to find something suitable, and I thought I'd go for a change this time. Something a bit more jazzy.'

'No, no, it's great,' I said. I really didn't want to hurt my sister's feelings, and annoyingly I'd turned into a bit of a people-pleaser over the years, probably to have an easy life, so I find it very hard to say what I actually think at the best of times. I used to be much more forthright... I picked up a box of Dairy Milk and a pot plant. 'Listen, you look fab. Go and have a wonderful evening with Henry, and Bella will be absolutely fine with us. Eat these chocolates for pudding. Thanks again for getting me a new client.'

'Thanks so much, Polly,' Marie said. 'And it's really sweet of you to give me these.' She held up the chocolates and plant. 'Oh, Bella's got a bag with her, it's got her school uniform in it for tomorrow morning.'

I nodded and waved my sister off. As I turned to go back into the house, a sudden thought struck me. *Oh God, was my sister entering a midlife crisis? I mean, she was pushing forty-five, isn't that prime crisis time? Shit. Perhaps that red dress was a warning sign. Maybe I should have a chat with her soon, make sure that she's feeling okay.* Because despite what I'd said to Marie, that dress she had on really didn't suit her. It made her look like the old woman I'd seen in Top Shop when I was twenty, who'd been stuffing herself into a boob tube; the one I'd felt so sorry for. My sister's choice of outfit was very out of character. And what other reason could there be for her dressing like that other than an impending midlife breakdown?

I'd talk to her soon, I decided. But now it was time to start preparing the jacket potatoes with cheese and beans that Danny had been adamant we should all have for dinner that evening. Pondering my sister's life choices would have to wait...

Chapter Thirteen

I sat back, watching Danny and Bella playing the board game Ludo on the carpet in front of me. My house was so tiny that it was a bit of a squish – the three of us in the living room together – but none of us minded. *Children never noticed things like that anyway*, I mused, as Danny yelped in mock frustration when Bella rolled a six with the dice. *We could be living in a shed and they'd still have fun. It was so good for him to have her over like this. Perhaps I should suggest to Marie that we got the children together on an even more regular basis, although with the hectic schedule she had them both on she might not have the time for that.*

My thoughts went back to the dress that my sister had been wearing. Was it me, or had there been little signs that her behaviour was changing slightly – aside from wearing that midlife crisis outfit today? Like when she'd forgotten that Oliver was still awake and just left the house to go and buy bread? *Hmm*, I thought. I was suddenly remembering a conversation we'd had on the phone a few weeks ago, before I got this job with Sylvie. I was moaning about my lack of funds to Marie, again, and she'd said something that I hadn't taken much notice of at the time.

'Well, Polly,' she'd said. 'I reckon that if Henry and I ever got to the point where we were going to lose our house, I'd do absolutely anything to keep us afloat. Sometimes you have to think outside the box in these sort of situations, you know? I mean, we're not exactly as flush as we have been at the moment, and I've been thinking about different ways that I could make some money. I've thought about all sorts of things, like taking up some sort of profession that pays to train like teaching – although if I'm honest I'd probably kill the little buggers after a couple of days if they started playing up. Or even doing something that the training is quite quick for, like hypnotherapy or massage work. I could do both of those from home. Why don't you broaden your horizons a bit, and think about other things that you can do? There's more to life than just tapping away at your laptop, you know.'

I'd just laughed and dismissed what she said at the time, and didn't think anything more about it afterwards. Until now. The thought of being anything other than a writer was alien to me. It was in my veins, it's what I did. I didn't think I could do anything else – very well, anyway. The thought of Marie being a teacher made me smile; she was a good mum to her own two kids, but had zero patience with anyone else's. And hypnotherapy? Maybe, but she'd never shown any interest in it before. Massage work? Wasn't that a euphemism for prostitution? Yeah right, like that would ever happen. She and Henry were the tightest, happiest couple that I knew. And although my sister could be bolshy and pig-headed at times, she also had good moral standards. But it was interesting that she was actually thinking about getting a job. She'd not mentioned applying for work since uber-rich Henry came on the scene. Maybe she just needed more freedom, to flex her wings after being a stay-at-home mum for so long? Help out with their cash-flow crisis a bit?

'Mummy?' Danny's words snapped me out of my reverie. 'Bella's won. Can we get the chess set out? I want to beat her at something before I go to bed.'

I laughed.

'Do you remember that we've been talking about being a good sportsman?' I reminded him. One downside of being an only child was that my son felt it was his natural right to win any game he played, probably because I'd made the mistake of letting him win when it was just him and me that played. 'Say "well done" to Bella, and I'll go and dig the chess set out of the cupboard.'

I heaved myself up out of the comfy sofa, and left Danny staring doubtfully at his cousin while I opened the messy cupboard in the corner of the living room. I couldn't help hoping that this chess game made them both mentally – and physically – tired, as I wanted at least a couple of hours that evening to finish writing up Sylvie's next instalment. The book wouldn't produce itself, and I was rather enjoying seeing her payments arrive in my account...

Chapter Fourteen

'How did the night out with Henry's work colleagues go?' I said. It was two days later, and I'd phoned my sister, hoping to subtly ask her how she was, and if there was anything else on her mind other than money worries. I couldn't really ask outright if she was having a midlife crisis, but that's what I wanted to get at. *Doctors could do amazing things for women with HRT now, couldn't they? Maybe a bit of oestrogen gel was all that my sister needed to start feeling a bit more on top of things again...*

'What?' Marie said. She'd sounded a bit distracted since she'd picked up the phone. 'Oh that. Well, you know how these things are.' *Nope,* I thought. *No idea. Never been to one.* 'Boring,' she went on. 'Same old twittering wives and puffed up important banking husbands. To be honest, I just enjoyed the wine mostly, as I knew we would be getting a taxi home after. Had quite a few glasses actually. Bit of a fuzzy head the next day.'

'Oh well, at least you had a nice meal and some wine for free,' I said. 'So it wasn't all bad. Everything all right with you, in general I mean?' *Like why are you suddenly wearing weirdly small dresses?* I added in my head. *It's kind of weird...*

'Yeah, good,' Marie said, sounding a bit vague, like she was trying to concentrate on something else at the same time as talking to me. 'Our money issues have eased a bit, so we're not panicking quite so much at the moment. Not out of the woods yet, but getting there.'

'Brilliant,' I said. I was very glad to hear that things were on the up for her and Henry. Not that they'd been that bad in the first place, really. *I'm not getting anywhere fast with the conversation*, I thought. *My sister obviously isn't in a chatty mood today. Which isn't like her, although I have to admit she's not been herself recently...*

I tried to engage Marie for a few more minutes, asking about the children, how they were getting on at school, general chit-chat sort of openers, but it soon became clear that she just wasn't interested in saying much. *Probably busy doing something else*, I decided. *She usually is these days.*

We said our goodbyes and I put my phone back in my pocket.

Maybe I'm worrying too much, I thought. *Perhaps Marie is absolutely fine. She's obviously got a lot on at the moment, what with one thing and another. Maybe she just wants to look a bit younger nowadays, hence her change in style. And there's nothing wrong with that, is there? Mum always said I was an over-worrier...*

But as I stood up to go and put the kettle on, something inside me – that I couldn't quite put my finger on – just didn't feel quite right about my sister...

Chapter Fifteen

Sylvie, Antoni and I worked hard on the book over the next couple of weeks. I felt like I was getting to know him better, and was trusting him more and more each time. He was obviously an intelligent man, and had loads of great ideas. He'd been brutally honest when we'd gone back in the story a bit so that he could fill me in on his bad boy ways in Poland, explaining how he'd had his first taste of drugs – marijuana – aged ten, and how he'd gone on to take speed after that.

'I could feel myself changing from that moment on,' Antoni had said. 'I don't know if you've ever taken drugs, Polly?' I shook my head. 'But they start eating away at your soul. Taking away the good bits. Making you act like a total wanker. I was in a lot of pain after my dad left, and I chose to deal with it the wrong way. Numb it with substances. Which made my behaviour worse.'

I respected his honesty, and had to admit that his input was giving our wonderful book more grit. So as I walked towards Sylvie's house for yet another interview, Dictaphone at the ready, I was looking forward to seeing them both. I hadn't directly asked, but I could tell – by that point – that they'd rekindled their romance. The way they looked at each other, spoke to each other, held each other's hands all made this fact obvious. Good for them, I thought. What a happy ending this will make to the book. That these two human beings have been through so much pain, yet have ended up growing together again.

But when Sylvie opened the door, I was shocked by the change that I saw in her. It had been four days since we'd last met, as I'd needed time to write up the latest instalment. And in that time, she'd become noticeably thinner, had bags under her eyes, and was looking distinctly less happy and glowing than she had been since Antoni got out of prison. And her house was no longer as spick and span as it usually was. There were belongings strewn across the floor and stains on the small hall table. Not that I was complaining about that – I mean, who was I to talk? It was just a noticeable difference that made an edge of concern creep into my brain.

When I walked into the living room I saw that Antoni was perched on the edge of the sofa, rolling a cigarette. Which was strange, as he'd told me many times about how he'd stopped smoking while he was in prison, as well as kicking his drug habit.

'Can't allow myself to be addicted to anything nowadays,' he'd told me in the past. 'With me, one thing just leads to another if I allow it. Addictive personality, you see?'

And when he glanced up at me as I entered the living room, he didn't smile like he normally did. I noticed that his foot was tapping agitatedly against the floor. *Hmm,* I thought. *There's a very different atmosphere in here today and it's not a nice one. I wonder if anything's happened between the two of them? I really hope not. It's none of your business, Polly,* I immediately told myself. *Stop getting so involved with your client's life and just get on with your job, for God's sake.*

There was a weird smell in the room, and I tried not to let

my nose wrinkle up because of it. It was a kind of burning plastic stench. It was pungent and it wasn't something I was enjoying breathing in at all. But I didn't know what was causing it and I didn't want to seem rude by asking about it, so I just sat there quietly until Sylvie came in with a tray of coffees. The tray was wobbling a bit, and some of the liquid slopped over the side of the mugs.

'Hey,' Antoni said sharply. 'Be more careful next time, Sylvie.'

She didn't say anything, just handed out the drinks and sat down next to him, squashing herself into the corner of the sofa. *What?* I thought. *Did he really just speak to her like that? Hang on a minute, what's going on here?*

'Right,' I said, trying to break the obvious tension in the room. 'Let's get started. Sylvie, can you tell me a bit more about what life was like for you once you and Antoni had reconnected in the UK? We've touched on that but I think we need to go into more detail about how it was that you two moved in with each other, if that's okay?'

'Er, yes, sure,' Sylvie said. Her eyes had been trained on the floor, but now she lifted them and met my gaze. She looked like she hadn't slept well for a few nights, poor thing. I had the sudden feeling that I wanted to get her on her own somehow, ask her what was going on. What had changed. Why Antoni clearly wasn't happy. And what the hell that disgusting smell was. 'So as I told you last time, when Antoni and I first got back together, everything was wonderful for a while.'

Out of the corner of my eye I could see Antoni nodding his head up and down.

'And we had some great times together then; on my days off we would explore London, you know, see the sights. Once, we took an open-top bus around the city, and saw everything – Buckingham Palace, the Houses of Parliament, the Tower of

London. We walked along the River Thames, and went for a drink on a barge there that's kind of like a floating pub. Then we made our way to Chinatown, got ourselves a delicious buffet, and went to eat it on the green in Soho. That was a great day. Good memories.'

She stopped and gave a big sigh.

'And then,' Sylvie went on, speaking slowly now, 'things became a bit stressful. Because although I was so glad that the chemistry between us had resurfaced, and we were spending lots of time together, one day I found a packet of white powder in one of Antoni's pockets...'

'Hey,' Antoni interrupted her, his tone aggressive. 'How many times do I have to tell you, Sylvie? I only used the cocaine to keep me awake at work. When you're on building sites you need all the energy you can get. It's hard labour, you know. Don't make it sound like I was doing anything wrong, okay?'

'Yes, I know what you've told me.' Sylvie's gaze was back on the floor.

Antoni shot her a dirty look, then fumbled in his pocket for something. He pulled out an inhaler. I noticed that the end of it was all burnt.

'Woah,' I said. 'Hey listen, Antoni. Please don't talk to Sylvie like that, okay? We've all been working really well on this book together, and we had an agreement that you could both speak openly and honestly about everything that has gone on before. If you start correcting Sylvie about things then it's just not going to work, is it? And remember, the idea is that this book is an inspiration, it's going to be Sylvie's amazing and powerful story, about how she overcame adversity and built up a good life. Let's keep that in mind. All right?' *Yes Polly,* I thought. *Just you let that assertiveness come out.*

Antoni shot me a look. His eyes were hard.

'Sorry,' he said. 'I won't interrupt again. Go on, Sylvie.'

'Well,' Sylvie said, her voice now a monotone. 'After that incident, things began to change between us. Listen, I'm sorry, Antoni,' she turned towards him, 'but I'm going to have to tell Polly about your drug dealing. It's part of the past. And I wanted to be really honest in this book.'

Antoni let out a stream of words – in Polish – that I didn't understand, but I knew were angry and aggressive. Every time Sylvie tried to answer him he bulldozed over her with more ranting. I fiddled with my Dictaphone, suddenly feeling very uncomfortable.

When his torrent of words had finally subsided, Sylvie turned to me. She had tears in her eyes.

'I'm so sorry, Polly, but I think we're going to have to call it a day. I can't go on with the interview right now. It's just not going to work at the moment. Let me show you out.'

As I walked out of her front door, glad to be getting away from the toxic atmosphere in her house, but now genuinely worried about Sylvie and the effect that Antoni was having on her life, I could hear his footsteps following us. Clearly she wasn't going to be allowed one minute of alone time with me. I couldn't believe what was happening. My worst fears, the niggling doubt about Antoni that I'd tried so hard to push away but that had never quite gone, was back in full force. This was the first time that I'd seen the aggressive side of him, the dangerous side, and it wasn't a nice thing to witness. I wasn't stupid, I couldn't ignore the fact that his mood had totally changed, the way he'd been rolling a cigarette, the horrible smell in the room, the burnt inhaler... Had he started taking drugs again?

'I'll be in touch,' Sylvie called after me as I walked towards my car. 'Very soon, I promise. I'm so sorry about this, Polly.'

As I turned to wave goodbye to her, I saw Antoni standing next to her. He looked angry.

As I started my car and drove away, the anger that had been building inside me as I'd watched Antoni control the woman I'd come to respect and like caused me to let out a loud growl. I thumped the steering wheel. *How dare he act like this? Hadn't he destroyed her life enough once before? Why hadn't I said even more to defend her?* It was too much, seeing another human being treated like shit. Clearly that stuff about him changing had only applied to when he was clean. If he'd started taking drugs again, that would explain his personality transplant, how he'd gone from seeming like a nice helpful guy, to acting like a dick. And I strongly suspected that that's exactly what had happened. Right, that was it. I was going to call an emergency meeting with Marie. And I desperately needed to meet with Sylvie on her own. Something needed to be done about this situation. Sylvie wasn't just my client now, she was a good friend. And there was no way that I was going to sit back and watch her dreams and life be disrupted by Antoni like this...

Chapter Sixteen

The rest of the afternoon passed quickly. I collected Danny from school, we went to the supermarket and I let him push the trolley, which he loved doing. I had to reach over and steer it away from other people's ankles a couple of times.

'Ooh, Mummy,' he said. 'Mummy? Can we get some doughnuts for pudding?'

'What?' I said as his words jogged me out of my thoughts about Sylvie. I couldn't concentrate properly, I'd been really shaken up by Antoni's behaviour. I'd tried calling my sister but she hadn't answered, so I'd sent her a text asking her to phone me ASAP. I'd sent a message to Sylvie, saying that the two of us needed to meet somewhere private, but she hadn't replied yet. 'Sorry, darling, what did you say?' I looked down at my son. 'Doughnuts? Yes, as long as you promise to eat all of your dinner first. Okay?' I have to say that I was enjoying being able to treat my son, now I was earning. He'd had to have plain budget biscuits as dessert for a long time now, and while that was fine and he rarely complained, it felt good to be able to buy more exciting things for him. Marie's cupboards always looked like a Waitrose store unit, they were generally jam-packed with mouth-wateringly delicious treats. And while I wasn't jealous of her social life, I'd been rather envious – on more than one occasion – of the variety of food she was always able to afford.

'Yep,' Danny said, going over to survey the sticky selection, his eyes now wide.

When we got home, I put the doughnuts to one side and made us some lasagne, while Danny watched his favourite TV show, *Dinotrux*. My time with Sylvie and Antoni kept replaying itself in my head, and I knew that I badly needed to talk to my sister about what was going on but I was just getting radio silence from her. As I layered the pasta sheets I wondered how I'd react if the man I was in love with was released from prison and wheedled his way back into my life, with promises about how he'd changed for the better. I liked to think that I wouldn't allow it, but how could I be sure unless I was in the exact same position? It was all too easy to judge Sylvie for making a big mistake. And I didn't think I'd make the same choice. But perhaps she'd genuinely believed that he'd changed. *Do people ever really change,* I wondered, *once they'd reached such levels of violence?* I felt disappointed, and a bit stupid too. I'd trusted Antoni, been sucked in by his charm and talk. But if what I witnessed today was anything to go by, he hadn't changed. Not in the long term anyway. Perhaps he'd genuinely tried to, for a bit. But then had got hold of some more drugs...

I remembered a documentary that I'd watched once, about ex-gang members who were now trying to do good in their communities. It included an interview with a man who'd shot people and been shot himself in the past, but who now ran a youth club for young people as he wanted to show them that there was a different way to be in life. That they didn't have to just follow what everyone else did to be accepted. Perhaps Sylvie had been hoping that Antoni had undergone some sort of similar transformation. It wasn't impossible. But if Antoni had

had genuine thoughts of changing his ways, he'd failed pretty quickly. *Maybe he only knows how to be like that,* I thought. *To take drugs, to control people, to make others around him be fearful of him. He's been doing it for so long, maybe it's literally impossible for him to change his ways?*

Well, I decided. *He was certainly never going to have that kind of hold over me!*

Chapter Seventeen

It was half nine that evening, and Danny was sleeping soundly upstairs in bed. Marie still hadn't replied to any of my messages, which was unusual. I desperately wanted to talk to her about Sylvie, and her silence was beyond frustrating. I tried ringing her again, but the phone just rang until it went to voicemail. Starting to get a bit worried, I texted Henry, just to make sure that everything was okay.

Yes fine, he messaged back. *Marie's gone out with some friends this evening. She's probably in a bad signal area or something.*

I didn't have any ghostwriting material that I could get on with, as Antoni had basically sabotaged the last meeting. To take my mind off everything that was going on, I decided to open up my laptop and take another look at the crime fiction novel I'd been writing – a psychological thriller – set on the Somerset coast, Kilve Beach to be exact, where Danny and I had spent a very fun long weekend during the summer holidays the previous year. The beach was so wild and barren-looking, that as I'd stared at it while Danny hunted for crabs among the rocks, a possible plot line had come to me. About a murder in a small, isolated coastal village, and how the locals wouldn't talk. How the murderer turned out to be the person everyone least expected, the popular landlord of the pub. I'd been trying to write the story ever since, but had only got to chapter five. I always put the ghostwriting jobs that I got before my own work, as after all, they paid the bills. I'd got a very decent whack for the bestselling one, although it had since dwindled away on the boring household expenses that everyone has to pay. And I was often too tired in the evenings, once I'd given Danny dinner, played with him and then put him to bed. But I had such a yearning inside me to be a published author in my own right. I really wanted to pen such a fantastic novel, that an agent or publisher snapped it up and told me how brilliant it was. I'd imagined – many times – how it would feel to see my own book baby, my work of art, rising up the charts. But up until now, I'd only managed to get short stories published. Which was still fantastic, I quickly reminded myself. I was very proud of the fact that I was at least in print. But a whole novel of my own – out in the world – would be so fabulous. And if it was successful it would really help with the money side of things...

My mobile bleeped into life just as I was imagining my successful crime book winning some sort of prestigious award. *Marie?* I thought, quickly grabbing my phone. *At last.* I looked at the number that was flashing on the screen, and then blinked. It was Jakub, Danny's father. Now this was unusual. He never phoned me nowadays, we always communicated about our son via text, it was just emotionally easier for us both. The break-up – while nothing like Sylvie and Antoni's – had been fairly unpleasant in terms of having to say goodbye to each other. We'd become friends but not lovers in the end, and had both realised that we were too young to carry on living like that. Things had happened at the end that I preferred not to think about, horrible things... But I'd still had to cope with that aching feeling of loss, the final ending, when we'd eventually gone our separate ways. And anyway, Jakub had moved to Norfolk two years ago, so that's why he hadn't seen his son since. Which, yes, was a poor reason, but still a reason nonetheless and was why he relied on my text updates about Danny and how he was doing. I couldn't even remember the last time that I actually spoke to him. *Was everything okay?*

'Hello?' I said, answering the phone quickly. 'Jakub?'

'Polly?' Jakub's husky voice said.

'Yes,' I said. 'Hi, how are you? It's been so long since we actually spoke. This is kind of strange.'

'Yes, I know,' Jakub said. He sounded strained. 'I'm sorry to phone you this late in the evening, but I need to discuss something with you, Poll.' Only Jakub and Marie ever called me Poll. And it was weird to hear him say it again. It made me feel quite emotional.

'Oh right?' I said. 'What's that then?'

I could hear a woman say something to Jakub in the background. Her voice sounded harsh, like she was giving him instructions.

'Yes I know, I know,' Jakub said, obviously to her. 'Give me a chance, will you? Sorry,' he said to me. 'This is a bit of a tricky thing to bring up, Poll. But it's about money.'

Oh God, I thought, my stomach sinking. I was hoping that we'd sorted all of that side of things out when we broke up. I'd had to admit to myself, after the break-up, that one of my main weaknesses in life had been handling money well. I was much better now, I'd forced myself to concentrate hard on saving money, and making sure the mortgage and bills were up to date. And if they weren't, I tried to find new jobs as soon as I could so that I could pay off the debts quickly. But back when Jakub and I had been together, when I was still a youngish and enthusiastic wannabe writer, I'd been in charge of paying the bills while he'd paid the rent of the small studio apartment we were living in at the time. But even with all that, Jakub was worse than me with finances, and I'd ended up lending – actually giving – him a lot of money here and there. He could be so persuasive. He'd barely paid me back anything, and in the end I'd resigned myself to the fact that he never would. I was older and wiser now, and never lent anyone my hard-earned cash. I'd learned that lesson the hard way. So why the fuck was he here to talk about money again?

'Er, yes?' I said, closing my eyes and waiting for the inevitable request for cash. I was still not in a great position myself financially. I'd managed to pay the bills I needed to with the ghostwriting money that Sylvie had transferred, but it was nearly the end of the month and more would be due soon. And what with Antoni's interference, the writing process was no longer running as smoothly and regularly as I'd have liked, so goodness knows when she'd next pay me...

'Tell her,' I heard a female voice hiss at Jakub in the background.

'Well,' he said, sounding very awkward. 'I'm really sorry to ask you this, Poll, but I'm in desperate need of money. It's for something really important; medical related actually. Could you possibly lend me five hundred? And I don't suppose there's any chance that you could transfer it this week, is there?'

I'd nearly dropped the phone when he'd said the amount. Five hundred? A spark of anger that had jumped into life in me was getting bigger. The bloody cheek of the man. What about everything I spent on our son, Jakub's child? Surely that had amounted to dozens of times more than this sum, and he had hardly contributed anything financially for Danny since the break-up. Something to do with his mental health, apparently he was finding it hard to hold a job down. And he had the actual gall to ask me for more money, after all this time? After he never paid anything back in the first place? When he couldn't even contribute financially towards the upkeep of his own child?

'Well,' I said. 'As you haven't sent any child maintenance for over two years, Jakub, and never paid me back for any of the loans I gave you when we were together, it seems kind of ridiculous to ask me for more money, doesn't it?'

Jakub let out a long sigh. I could hear the woman's voice in the background getting more frantic, although I could no longer hear exactly what she was saying, as though she'd moved further away from his phone.

'I do understand what you're saying,' Jakub said. 'But I really need that money, Polly. I'll be able to tell you why soon, but just trust me, I kind of really need you to transfer it to me this week. All I can say at the moment is that it's for something medical.'

What the fuck? I thought. *Was he mad – suddenly demanding this of me? And anyway, what was the rush? Jakub knew I was very far from flush, and it was extremely unusual for him to phone up and demand cash straight away like this...*

'I don't have that kind of money right now,' I said, my tone becoming sharp. 'As you well know. Danny and I lead a very hand-to-mouth existence at the best of times. So the answer is a firm no.' Even though I was pissed off, it was so good to feel a tiny bit of my former feistiness returning.

I knew I needed to ring off at that point, as I didn't want to get into an argument with the father of my child over something so stupid. I hadn't spoken to him for ages, and I was feeling too tired and stressed about Sylvie to get into a problem with him over the phone.

The woman he'd been with sounded like hard work, I reflected as I put my phone down, closed my laptop and then trudged up the stairs towards my bedroom. I was going to call it a night, I was now too annoyed to get any writing done. Not that it was any of my business who he was with, and I no longer cared about Jakub dating other people. Genuinely. In fact, relationships were starting to look too stressful – if Sylvie and Jakub were anything to go by. No, I was quite happy keeping it just me and Danny for the time being. Leading a peaceful life was fine by me and I loved being on my own in the evenings. Had even started wondering whether Danny and I should get a cat, as they were low maintenance and looked after themselves, but provided some sort of company – on their terms, just like me. But it was strange that Jakub had chosen to be with such a demanding-sounding woman. He was usually quite a chilled person. I couldn't help wondering what on earth had attracted him to her. It was very out of character for him to put up with being treated like that...

Chapter Eighteen

Marie finally got back to me at half past nine the next morning, just after I'd got back from dropping Danny at school.

'Sorry, sis,' she said. 'It's been a bit mental here, so busy. But then it always is. What can I do for you?'

Rather than try and explain everything about Sylvie and Antoni to Marie over the phone, I asked if she could spare ten minutes to come round to my house and have a chat. It would be much easier if we could speak face to face, I'd decided, as then I'd be able to tell if I was getting the message across right about the impact that Antoni was having on poor Sylvie. Things could get confused over a phone call.

'Ah, okay,' she said, not sounding overly thrilled. 'But I have to leave by half ten, if that's all right, Polly. I've got the hairdressers at eleven, and I can't miss the appointment as my roots are awful now. I'm starting to look like a badger.'

It wasn't long before I heard my sister's car screech to a halt outside the house. She drove as she lived life, full on and unapologetically. Soon, we were sitting on either side of my little wooden kitchen table, with mugs of coffee in front of us.

'So,' Marie said. 'What's up, Poll? You look worried about something.'

I took a deep breath, then did my very best to explain the situation between Sylvie and Antoni to my sister. How she'd seemed before he'd got out of jail, how determined she'd been to write this book, how strong and independent she'd come across as. How happy she'd been when she'd reconnected with Antoni, and how charming and polite he'd been with her. And then her recent deterioration, how he'd started smoking again – possibly drugs. His hissy fit, his attitude. How she could no longer tell the tale as she'd first intended.

'It's just not right, Marie,' I said. 'I mean, I haven't known Sylvie for that long, but I hate seeing her treated like this by him. I really like her, she's such a lovely person. I couldn't bear watching Antoni speaking down to her; it was awful. And she's no longer able to freely tell me her life story. This book is really important; it's giving a voice to a survivor of abuse, yet now the same man who caused her all that pain is getting in the way of it. I really, really wish she'd never told him about the book, but it's done now, and I was wondering if you could help me see a way forward with it all. Is there any way we can help to protect Sylvie from Antoni?'

I sat back, and waited. If there was one person I knew who would be able to give me a good perspective on this, and tell me what the right thing to do would be, it was Marie. She'd always had an old head on her, even when we were little. Always talked sense into me if I'd got upset or anxious about something or other. And got me back on track after Mum died, convincing me that Mum would never want me to fall apart like I was doing, that she'd lived for us, and now she wanted us to live good lives for her. I'd listened to this advice, and had slowly been able to pull myself out of the rut that I was in.

'Ah,' my sister said. 'I see. Yes, I've also become aware that Antoni isn't having the best effect on Sylvie.'

'You have?' I said. I still wasn't sure how deep the friendship between Sylvie and Marie went, but I didn't think my sister knew much about Antoni. At least, that's what I'd presumed...

'Yes,' Marie said. 'The other night, when I was round at theirs...'

'Wait,' I said. 'You were at Sylvie's house at night-time? And Antoni was there? I thought that he was just coming over in the daytime when Filip was at school, because of what his parole officer said.'

'Yes,' Marie said. A strange expression flitted across her face, and it was one that I couldn't easily read. She was usually open about things, but it seemed that she wasn't going to elaborate much on this particular detail. 'Sylvie and I have become quite good friends really, Poll. We help each other out here and there.'

With what? I wanted to ask. *How can she help you out? I'm the one that you turn to when you need help with Bella or Oliver. In what way does Sylvie help you? Crikey, Polly,* I thought suddenly. *Are you turning into a jealous sister? Marie's allowed to have good friends, you know. Even if they do associate with violent criminals...*

I nodded, biting down all the questions that had arisen in my head.

'Antoni's a complicated character,' Marie went on. 'I think there is a nice side to him; there must be otherwise Sylvie wouldn't have got together with him in the first place. He's intelligent, quick-witted, and he can be very charming and caring. And she wouldn't have started meeting up with him again unless she was sure that he'd really changed, would she? She's also smart. And when I first got to know Antoni after he'd got out of jail, I was convinced as she was that he was a changed man. He just seemed so wise, so able to reflect on the past and what he'd done.'

When you first got to know Antoni? I thought. *So this is a regular thing? Shit, there's more going on here than I realised. Why hasn't Marie been more open with me about how close she and Sylvie are? I don't mind, but it seems a bit weird...*

'Right,' I said, nodding. 'But now that he's not being so sweet and charming, what's Antoni like when you're there?'

'Well,' Marie said. It was almost as though she was reluctant to admit how unpleasant the man could be. *Why on earth would she feel like that?* 'Unfortunately Antoni hasn't had a very good life. As I'm sure Sylvie must have told you, his dad left the family when he was young, and his mother couldn't cope with all her children. He was left to run wild on the streets. He's brought himself up the best way that he can, but he doesn't always get it right, Polly. He's made big mistakes in the past, and he's paid for them big time. Since I've got to know him, he's said so many times that he wants a different life now. That he just wants to be normal and stay out of trouble. It can't be easy, completely changing your ways once you're out in the big wide world again, can it? I mean, he definitely has good intentions, but I think he has hit a rocky patch, where the reality of how he has to behave in order to keep living a good life is dawning on him. There's bound to be some bad days, as he eases himself into his new free life. It's not like in films, when people have a complete transformation in a couple of days. This is real life, Polly, and it's going to take Antoni a while to settle back into it.'

'But,' I said, feeling confused. *Was it me, or did it sound like Marie was almost defending Antoni? Trying to justify and minimise his behaviour? Or perhaps just being wilfully blind to the recent developments with him?* 'That's all very well, and I understand that he needs time to settle back into life. I get the fact that it won't be an easy ride for him, and that he will make mistakes along the way. But isn't there a difference between doing that and starting to take drugs again? Especially if his former abusive behaviour was massively affected by his crack use? What if he's made the choice to start smoking it again and has lost his focus on changing for the better?'

'Listen,' Marie said, her tone suddenly sounding edgy. She leaned towards me across the table. 'Let's get real here for a minute. Do you want this writing job or not, Polly? Do you want to earn some good money so that you can look after yourself and Danny? Or do you want to have to get a job outside the house with long hours, and hardly ever get to see your son? I put you in touch with Sylvie in good faith. You've known from the start – when you met her in her bistro for the first time – that she's led a complex life. One that involves violence, gangs, drugs and criminals. But you chose to go ahead with the job. You've given her your word that you'll write this book. So one way or another, unless you want to go back to being extremely poor, just stop being so judgemental about her and Antoni's relationship and get on with finishing it. Okay?'

And with that, Marie stood up. Her cheeks were flushed now. *Wow*, I thought. *What a strange response she's had to what I said. I never saw that one coming. I thought she'd totally understand, especially as she seems to be such good friends with Sylvie. It's almost like she's got something to lose by me rocking the boat here and trying to get Sylvie away from Antoni. Although that seems ridiculous. Or maybe she's actually right, and telling me a truth that I don't want to hear?*

'Marie,' I said, trying to keep my tone soothing. 'Please, sit down. I didn't mean to aggravate you with what I said, I'm simply a bit worried about the way Antoni's treating Sylvie. I just wanted to run my thoughts by you and see what your take on it all was. Can we maybe discuss this a bit more?'

'No, I've got to go,' my sister said, heading for the door. She seemed a bit rattled today, and even when she'd arrived she'd seemed distracted as though her head was somewhere else.

'Okay,' I said, standing up. My sister was very stubborn, once she'd decided to do something there would be no talking her out of it, I knew this from past experience. 'I'll show you out.'

'Bye, Polly,' Marie said, as she opened the front door and walked towards her car. 'And remember what I said. You've got a chance to make good money here. Don't mess it up.'

And with that, she was gone.

As I closed the front door, my thoughts were spinning. *Did all that really happen?* I wondered, exhaling and slithering down into a kitchen chair.

Chapter Nineteen

The rest of the morning passed uneventfully after that, with my conversation with Marie going round and round in my head. After a while, I began to soothe myself with the thought that she was probably just under a lot of financial pressure, and as a result wasn't acting like she normally did. Worry could make people snappy, couldn't it? Maybe this hadn't been the best time to ask her advice about Sylvie. Perhaps I should just leave her alone for a little while; give her a chance to sort things out at home. And maybe I should consider that – despite her edgy manner – she might have actually been giving me some good advice...

Brigitte, I thought, an image of my wonderful friend popping into my head. *She'd give me a good perspective on it all.* And she was nothing like my sister, my friend had always been so calm and level-headed. She was never one to snap at people. I picked up my phone and fired a text off to her, explaining the situation, how my new ghostwriting client was now being hassled and controlled by her ex-con boyfriend who she'd got back in touch with after he was let out of prison. Ten minutes later, my phone pinged.

Oh, this sounds like a serious situation, Polly, Brigitte had written. *I had no idea that Antoni was actually out of jail now.*

Hmm, I thought. *Had I not told her about that bit?* We'd had texts flying back and forth since I'd taken on this job, but everything had become so busy lately I couldn't remember what I'd told her and what I hadn't. And perhaps I'd wanted her not to worry about anything, making it appear like it was all still going well.

It sounds awful for Sylvie, Brigitte wrote. *I'd hate to be in her position. Can't she just break off contact with him? And, Polly, make sure you keep yourself safe. This job sounds like it's taken a worrying turn. Don't get too involved if things are getting dangerous, okay?*

Yep, I thought, *it most definitely has. So on the one hand, I had my sister advising me to shut up and carry on writing to earn the money, and I had Brigitte telling me that the whole thing didn't sound great and to be careful and not to get too involved. But who was right? Who did I agree with more?* I thought. As my vision wandered around the room, I caught sight of the messy pile of bills in the corner. *Hmm, I still had these bloody things to pay. So maybe I needed to take Marie's advice and just get on with it, while taking Brigitte's words seriously, and being as cautious as I could...*

I tried to write a bit more of my thriller, but my mind kept going back to Marie and Brigitte's conflicting opinions, and to poor Sylvie and the predicament she was in. My natural reaction was to step in and help her. But was this wise? Was I overstepping some professional line? I couldn't concentrate on my manuscript, I wasn't writing anything good, so I shut my laptop and stood up to fix myself a bowl of soup. As I walked across the kitchen to the fridge, my phone – which was in the pocket of my jeans – burst into life. I retrieved it, and looked at the name of the person calling. Sylvie.

'Hello?' I said.

'Polly,' Sylvie said. She was half-whispering. 'I know this is short notice, but is there any way you can come and meet me somewhere now? There's a few things I need to explain to you. Antoni has gone out with his friends for the afternoon, but it's still better if you don't come to my house in case he comes back unexpectedly or something. Can I meet you by the Crystal Palace War Memorial in about half an hour, and maybe we can go for a walk together? Somewhere quiet where we can chat?'

'Yes, sure, that's fine,' I said. Despite what my sister had said to me, I was relieved that I'd finally get some time alone with Sylvie, but an edge of concern had also crept into my brain. *What if she was going to call off the book altogether? What if Antoni had exerted even more power over her and told her that she could no longer go on with it?* My whole new source of income would completely stop, and while I felt rather selfish for thinking this given what Sylvie was going through, it was a real worry nevertheless. And my dreams of going on the creative writing course, using it as a stepping stone to success, I really didn't want to say goodbye to that course of action... *Oh why had he been paroled just when we'd started to write this book together? And why had she got back in contact with him? There is no point bemoaning these things,* I told myself, *as the fact is that they'd both happened. What was important was how we chose to go forward from here...*

We said our goodbyes, and I hurried around the house getting ready to leave. I'd have to come straight back and pick Danny up after I'd talked to Sylvie, I realised, so I grabbed a snack and a drink for him to have on the way home. I'd learned that doing this kept him in a much better mood for the evening ahead – which made both our lives easier.

Twenty-five minutes later, I'd somehow found a parking space in busy Crystal Palace, and was making my way towards the War Memorial. Sylvie was already there. I could only see her profile, but she looked like a shadow of the woman I'd met for the first time in the bistro. Thinner, hunched. As though the light in her was diminishing. *It was incredible how much someone could change in just a few short weeks*, I reflected, as I approached her. *It's such a sad thing to witness.*

'Hi, Sylvie,' I said.

'Oh, Polly,' she said, turning. I saw the dark bags under her eyes. 'Thanks so much for coming to meet me. Shall we cross the road and go for a walk in the park?'

'Yes, good idea,' I said. We set off.

'I'm so sorry about Antoni's behaviour when you were last at my house,' Sylvie said. I looked across at her and her expression was one of pure misery. It was heartbreaking to see such a decline in her spirit. 'I truly believed that he was a changed man when he came out of prison. I promise you that, Polly. I would never have jeopardised my life and health and Filip's safety otherwise. And the chance to write this book with you. Antoni seemed to so genuinely want a new, normal life, to learn how to live well and be a good person. And to start with, he was back to being the loving man that I knew when we got together when he came over to England all those years ago. But now the nasty side of him started to come out again. His narcissism has returned, he's just so full of himself. And it's because he's started smoking crack again.'

My mouth fell open slightly. I couldn't help it.

'I also suspect he's begun dealing drugs again, although he won't tell me the truth about this and shouted in my face when I asked him. He's hanging around with his horrible old friends again too, the people he knew when he was active in the Palace City Boys. I can't believe it, I feel so stupid for having believed what he said; how he promised me that he'd given up drugs. He keeps telling me that they still think he's the king, that he's the top dog. He's so deluded, it frightens me.'

I winced inwardly. I'd suspected from the start that it was a bad idea for Sylvie to get close to Antoni again, and now all my worst fears were being confirmed. Part of me wanted to ask her how she could have been so stupid. The other part just felt sorry for this wonderful woman, who'd been played for a fool yet again.

'He told me that in prison it was hard to get hold of any,' Sylvie went on, 'and that he didn't like Spice – the one that's popular on the inside – so he'd got clean. One day, before the last time that you saw him, I knew he'd been smoking crack again, as there were white frothy bits round his mouth. That's a dead giveaway. His mood has been getting worse and worse since then. It's a nightmare now, Polly, and he's ignoring any boundaries I'm trying to set. He took my front door key and got another one cut for himself. He's told me not to even think about changing the locks, and I know what he's capable of, so I'm too scared to do that.'

I sighed. This was going from bad to worse to fucking awful.

'He likes coming round to my house because it's much nearer to his old mates. He hates living in Dagenham. He wasn't supposed to see Filip yet, but he violated that agreement too, and he just doesn't seem to care about Filip when he does see him, which is really upsetting my son.'

She shook her head.

'But...' I said, searching for the right words. I knew that I didn't fully understand as I hadn't lived the life that Sylvie had. I'd never been in love with Antoni, and I didn't have a child with him. 'Why don't you tell the police and the parole board about what he's doing, how he's acting and behaving? Then if they come and re-arrest him, you'll be free again and can stop seeing him altogether? It seems kind of obvious to me,' I said the words gently, 'that you need to break off all contact with him.'

Sylvie grimaced as we turned into the park.

'Oh believe me, I'd love to do that,' she said. 'But unfortunately things aren't quite so simple. Antoni's been lying to his parole officer since he's got out of prison, I've heard him on the phone to him recently, telling him how well he's doing and that he's stayed off the drugs. If I tell the police then all they will do is come and talk to him. They won't arrest him again, especially if they don't find any evidence of him having done anything wrong.'

She paused, and I realised I was shaking my head slowly. It was all so desperate. So hard to hear.

'And Antoni's not stupid,' she went on. 'He knows how to hide his crack use from people when he wants. He's always one step ahead of me. He's already told me that if I make life difficult for him in any way, he'll take our son, Filip, and move away with him. He said that he'll make sure I never see my son again. And I know what he's capable of, Polly. I'm so stupid, I can see now that I should have never met up with him again. But he sounded so different when I spoke to him that day on the phone when he was in jail. He was so loving, he sounded so genuine, like he'd really changed. I had all these ideas about how I could help him settle back into life on the outside. But I've found out the hard way that he's not actually changed at all. Maybe he did really want to live a better life at one point, but once he saw his old friends that was it. Back to his bad habits.'

'Oh God, Sylvie, that's awful,' I said. I was imagining how I'd feel if someone threatened to take Danny away from me. I realised that I'd do absolutely anything to keep my son safe. I was beginning to understand what a delicate and tricky situation Sylvie was in, and how she had to tread on eggshells with Antoni. 'I'm so sorry. I really want to do something to help you, but it sounds like it wouldn't be a good idea for me to go and speak to the police on your behalf?'

Sylvie's head snapped up.

'Oh no, please don't do that,' she said. 'It would make Antoni so angry, and they wouldn't lock him up or anything. They'd leave him out and free, and then I'd be the one to deal with his rage. And he'd be angry with you too, Polly. No, please don't ever do that.'

I sighed.

'Yep,' she said. 'It's a total nightmare. The only good thing is that I've arranged for Filip to go and stay with the Dabrowskis for the time being. You know, the family who gave me that cleaning job when I first came to the UK. They're very old now, but I explained a bit of the situation to them and they said they'd be happy to have him. I've told Antoni that Filip needs a break from seeing him. He agreed, because ultimately it's me he wants to control, not our son.'

I shook my head, speechless. It was such an awful situation, and my heart was aching for Sylvie, for how she must be feeling? How her life had changed since Antoni had got out of prison. He really was a vile human being. A parasite, who had no appreciation at all for what Sylvie had tried to do for him. He just took and took and gave her nothing back, except fear and misery.

'That's not all,' Sylvie said, as we walked past one of the giant dinosaur statues that Crystal Palace Park is so famous for. Danny was really into dinosaurs, but I couldn't make out which type this one was supposed to be. An Apatosaurus perhaps? I honestly had no idea. I held my breath. *Oh God*, I thought. *Was Sylvie about to call off our ghostwriting agreement?*

'As you know now,' Sylvie's voice sounded more strangled, 'it's become impossible for me to write the book the way I want to. Antoni is too controlling. So I suggested to him that I call the whole thing off...'

Boom, there it is.

'But he said no,' Sylvie said. *Wait, what?* I thought. 'He

basically wants the book written in a way that glorifies him and his gang life,' Sylvie went on. 'He's told me in great detail about what I'm supposed to say to you. He's actually very excited about the idea. He thinks it's going to make him famous – or infamous – in some way; like the great hardened criminal who's bragging about what he's done. He wants to be the most well-known gangster in London, and to make members from other gangs scared of him. I've told you he's grandiose and narcissistic – well, this is the result of it. He's always wanted to be immortalised forever as some sort of god to the people he thinks follow him, and now he thinks this is his best chance. He knows you wrote a bestseller before, and he's convinced that you'll do another just for him.'

'Right,' I said, exhaling. I couldn't believe my ears. I really needed this job, but I had professional boundaries. There was no way I could actually consider doing this. I'd have to let Sylvie down gently, explain that Antoni's vision here was ridiculous and that it just couldn't happen. To switch from writing an honest account about a courageous lady's life and survival of awful abuse, to bigging up the actual abuser, some wannabe gangster who I loathed? The idea was unthinkable. It called into question every ethical and moral part of me. The reason I'd been so excited about writing the book was because I'd wanted to help Sylvie get her powerful tale out into the world, to help inspire other abuse victims. The thought of suddenly switching it to glorifying her abuser made me feel physically ill.

'And,' Sylvie went on, 'Antoni has had what he thinks is the best idea yet. He wants you, me and him to hire a cottage in some remote part of the countryside, so we can go there and be uninterrupted for a while. He wants you to get this book written super quickly. All he sees are pound signs, when he thinks about it being for sale on Amazon. He's got such a big ego, that he thinks that tens of thousands of people will be rushing to their computers to buy it the day that it is published. He hasn't realised – despite me trying to tell him – that it takes a while to get a book published. That it's an uncertain and complex process at the best of times. But he's convinced himself – because of your past success – that soon he'll be the most famous, or infamous, man in Britain.'

I laughed, I couldn't help it.

'That's ridiculous, Sylvie,' I said. 'I mean, how can he seriously think this is a good idea? How can he believe that I'd ever consider doing it? He's living in la-la land. There's no way I'd ever write a book about an abusive man like Antoni. He tricked you into trusting him again, and now he's back to his old, vile habits. No way. I wanted to write the book for you because you're so amazing, and have gone through so much. I'd prefer to never write anything again, rather than write a book glorifying Antoni.'

'But, Polly, please listen.' Sylvie's voice was full of anguish, and when I looked at her I saw tears falling down her pale cheeks. 'I told him all that too, when he came up with this brainwave. I told him that you're a good person and that you'd never do it. Then he said, if you did write it for him, he'd get out of my life once and for all and leave me and Filip alone. He said once he had the completed manuscript – which he wants me to pay for – then I could change the locks on my door, and never see him again, if that's what I wanted. He sees this as a chance to make money, to be held up as a notorious gangster, and to regain respect on the streets.'

This time I didn't laugh. Things had suddenly become deadly serious. I wanted to help Sylvie so badly, I wanted to help her get away from her abuser. And she was now telling me that the way I could do this was to write a book about him? And his horrible behaviour? Jesus, this was a head fuck.

'But, Sylvie,' I continued, my voice wavering.

'Hypothetically, let's say I did agree to write the book and make it all about him. How do you know he's going to keep his promise to you afterwards? How do you know that once he has the completed manuscript he will then just leave you alone? He hasn't proved to be at all trustworthy so far, has he?'

Sylvie stopped walking. She looked like she was going to faint.

'No,' she said, her voice a whisper. 'No, I don't have any proof that he will keep his word, Polly. But it's the best chance I've got. He's ruining my life again. He took my trust and manipulated it, and I was so, so stupid for letting him do that. I can see it all so clearly now. Everything I've worked so hard for is now on the line. If he doesn't get this book done the way he wants it, I just know that Antoni will make my life a living hell. And he knows I'm too scared of him to go to the police. My business, my son, everything will be affected.'

She burst into tears, heavy, racking sobs suddenly taking over her body. I stepped over and gave her a tight hug, my own heart ripped and ready to explode in pain. Oh God, how had things come to this? I thought. How had our plans, to get this wonderful book out into the world, become so utterly fucked up – all because of one disgusting man? Did I have a part to play in this? I wondered. Maybe if I'd never agreed to write the book for Sylvie, then things wouldn't have got to this point. But how could I – or anyone – look into the future? I'd never have been able to have predicted that things would turn out like this. It never even crossed my mind that Antoni would be able to draw me into his manipulation of Sylvie, and basically say that I as a writer had the power to set her free from him. How could I – in all good faith – just walk away from Sylvie at this point? Maybe Antoni really would leave her alone if I wrote this goddamn book for him?

'I-I just need some time to think about all this, okay?' I said.

'It's a big change, a big turnaround of events. I really do want to help you, Sylvie, so much. It's just that writing the book for Antoni would be such a bad and unethical thing for me to do...'

'Oh *please* say yes.' Sylvie turned towards me, and as I stepped away I saw the desperation in her eyes. 'I know it's a huge thing to ask of you, and believe me, I normally would never expect you to do such a thing. But Antoni will blame me if you say no. He'll make my life a living hell. He will say it's my fault, and that I told you not to write his book. He will do such terrible things to me, Polly, and maybe even to Filip. He gets furious when he doesn't get his own way about something. And this is my one chance to get him out of my life for good. To be able to be free again, and to get back to concentrating on my son and my business. If Antoni stays in my life, it's as good as over. He'll probably end up trying to kill me again at some point in the future.'

I looked up at the sky. I felt trapped by her words. Her future safety was basically in my hands, and it would mean I had to do something that every fibre in my body was telling me to walk away from.

'I know it all sounds crazy,' she went on, 'and it will be hard for me to take a week off work but he wants me to go away with you both too, probably so that he can keep exercising his control over me until the last minute. I can get my manager, Jo Cox, to run the bistro for a while if we go. She's excellent at her job, and I know I'll be leaving the place in safe hands. Please help me with this, I just need to get him away from me.'

Fuck, I thought, staring at her. *Fuck, fuck, fuck.* I was in a really tricky situation here. I was suddenly being used as Sylvie's way 'out', as her point of freedom. Every bit of sense in me was trying to make me turn to Sylvie and say no, sorry, I can't do this...

'If you do this, come and stay with me and Antoni for a few

days and just get this book written, I'll pay you all the money that you're owed,' Sylvie said quickly, her words tumbling over each other. 'I have some savings, I'll pay you double what we originally agreed. How about it? It's good money, Polly. Oh, please, please say yes.' Tears were still flowing thick and fast down her cheeks. I'd never seen another human being look so utterly desperate before. And I had the chance to help her, to get this monster out of her life again... And the extra money would be good, no, scrap that, it would be great. I'd definitely be able to go on that writing course. The one I'd lusted after for so long...

'Fine,' I said, hardly able to believe the words that were coming out of my mouth. 'I'll come and stay with you and Antoni for a few days, and get this book written quickly, if you're sure that you want him taking it over and being written to glorify him. But I want him to write down his promise to you that he will get out of your life for good once I give him the completed manuscript, okay? That bit needs to be made official.'

'Oh thank you, Polly, thank you,' Sylvie said, wiping her eyes. 'You've literally saved my life. I'll be indebted to you forever, I know how hard this is and how much you don't want to do it. But you're giving me the chance to be free of Antoni, and it's so amazing of you. I'll tell him when he's finished doing whatever he's doing with his mates. The sooner we get this all over with, the quicker we can both get back to normal.'

I nodded, feeling dazed. *What the fuck had just happened? What on earth had I just agreed to?*

Chapter Twenty

'Dad?' I called. It was the next day, Saturday, and Danny and I had just arrived at my childhood house in Bromley – the sprawling town next to Beckenham – the one my dad insisted on living in even though his arthritis was bad now and he struggled to make it up the stairs each evening. Marie and I had both suggested that he sell up and move to a bungalow, but my dad – always quietly stubborn – wouldn't hear of it. I think he probably wanted to be where he could remember my mother the best, where he could picture her cooking in the kitchen, or taking the younger versions of us upstairs at bedtime. He'd never really got over her death, and he probably never would. I understood this, I desperately missed my mother too. But I had Danny to focus on, whereas he just had his memories.

'Dad?' I called again, rapping loudly on the dilapidated front door. Danny ran round the side of the house towards the back gate.

'Grandad,' he shouted. 'Where are you?'

I saw some movement through the obscured pane of glass in the front door. A jumbled silhouette coming nearer and nearer.

'He's here, Danny,' I said loudly. It took my father quite a bit of time to shuffle anywhere nowadays. My son bounded back and stood next to me.

'Hello, Polly, hello, Danny,' my dad said in his papery thin voice as he opened the front door. 'How nice to see you. Do come in.' He was wearing his usual attire, a tank top over a shirt, and chino trousers that no longer fitted as he'd lost so much weight recently.

Ten minutes later, my dad and I were sitting in his living room, with cups of tea in our hands. Danny was in his favourite place at Grandad's: the garden. Dad had once been a keen gardener, and had always been very green-fingered. He'd been able to cultivate beautiful flowers in the poorest types of soil. But since Mum died, and his joints got more painful, Dad's garden had slowly become a wilderness; a place of forgotten memories. Which wasn't as pretty to look at, but the upside was that my son thought it was the best place on earth to go adventuring in. It was full of ramshackle sheds and storage places, a willow whose branches swept the grass, piles of brambles, thick bushes and rows and rows of straggly plants and flowers. Danny called it 'the jungle', and had been overjoyed when he heard that we were going to Grandad's because it meant he'd have another chance to go exploring.

'How's life?' Dad said, his tone as quiet as ever. He took a sip of tea and waited for my reply. I felt like he was slipping away from me these days, he was even more reserved than he had been when I was growing up. Sometimes I felt like I was visiting someone else's father, not my own...

'It's good,' I said, wondering how to broach the subject of him having Danny for a few days. He'd never exactly been a hands-on grandad, although I knew he loved all his grandchildren very much. Being the active, involved grandparent just wasn't his style. 'My writing is going well, in fact, I've just taken on a really well-paid job, Dad. It's for a lady who has an absolutely cracking story to tell. Full of twists and turns. I think it's going to make a great read, actually.'

'Fantastic,' Dad said. 'I'm glad to hear it.' He took another sip of his tea.

'The thing is,' I said. 'The woman I'm writing the book for wants me to go away with her for a few days. She wants the manuscript written really quickly, you see. And she's asked if I could leave Danny with someone else, to give us a chance to get it all done and dusted as quickly as possible.' *Okay, so this was a little white lie. It was me choosing to leave Danny behind, as I didn't want him to be around Antoni, but I couldn't exactly say that. And what was Dad going to make of me acting with such unusual spontaneity? Would he smell a rat?*

Dad regarded me with his hooded, intelligent eyes.

'Right,' he said.

'And the thing is,' I went on, 'I can't really ask Marie, because she doesn't seem herself at the moment. I think she's worried about something. And I don't want to put any more stress on her, by asking if Danny can stay.'

Dad nodded.

'I was thinking the same about your sister,' he said. 'She came to see me the other day, and she seemed very distracted. Not herself at all. Do you have any idea what's troubling her, Polly? She wouldn't tell me anything when I asked.'

'No, not really,' I said, feeling a bit guilty. Marie and I had a rule that we wouldn't divulge each other's personal lives to Dad – we left it up to the individual to disclose what they wanted to him. It was because he'd seemed so down for a few years now, depressed even, and if we were going through a bad time we didn't want him to worry.

Dad nodded, but didn't say anything.

'So,' I said. 'I was wondering if there's any chance that Danny could come and stay with you for a few days, Dad. I wouldn't normally ask, it's just that this job is going to pay really well...'

Dad stared at me. I've always found it very hard to work out what he's thinking, and as he's a man of few words, he rarely tells me his thoughts himself. I knew I was acting in a way that he would think was unusual, but he was my only hope. If Marie had started leaving the children at home at night – for whatever reason – I wasn't really comfortable leaving my son with her anyway, notwithstanding her busy lifestyle...

'Who's the job for?' he said, eventually.

'Oh, just a friend of Marie's,' I said. 'A lady called Sylvie. She's lovely. She wants me to write down her life story for her. She's from Poland, and she moved over here years ago. She's led quite a colourful life, and has known some crazy people. She wants the whole project done super quickly so she can get the book published and start making money from it.' There was no point going into specifics about Antoni's criminal past, or the fact that Sylvie used to work as a prostitute. This kind of news would worry most parents, and Dad would probably try and talk me out of going to Wales with her then. And we'd only be gone a few days, and then if Antoni kept his word Sylvie would be free...

Dad nodded again.

'Yes,' he said. 'That's fine, Polly. I'll have young Danny to stay for a few days, I'd be glad to. It will be nice to have a child staying in the house again. And there's not much I can do to help you these days, so I would be happy to assist you with this, especially as it's for work.'

I breathed out. *Thank God for that.*

'Oh thanks, Dad, thanks so much,' I said. 'I know this is short notice, but I'll be leaving this coming Monday morning, and will be back on Friday evening. Is that okay? I'll come straight over and pick Danny up as soon as I can.' Sylvie had texted me the details about our impending trip the night before. Apparently she and Antoni had gone online as soon as he'd arrived back at her house. He'd picked out a cottage in Wales for us to stay in for the week. It had all been arranged so quickly. I didn't really understand why Antoni wanted us to go away to do it, maybe he thought I'd write extra fast if I had no distractions around and that this would help him quickly become a millionaire famous gangster overnight once the book was published?

Dad nodded.

'That's fine,' he said. 'If you drop Danny at school on Monday morning, I'll make sure I'm there to pick him up in the afternoon.'

I thanked him again, and we chatted on for a while about this and that; Dad's arthritis, the local church that he was involved with, the psychological thriller that I was trying – and failing – to write.

My phone pinged, and I fished it out of my pocket and stared at the text message that was flashing up on the screen. It was from my sister.

How exciting does Wales sound? my sister had written. *I'm coming too, Polly! Antoni invited me this morning. He said that you all needed transport, and that he didn't think your car or Sylvie's would be very comfortable to sit in for such a long journey. I could do with a break away, life at home is too stressful at the moment. I can't wait! Have a great weekend, and see you on Monday xxx*

What? I thought, suddenly feeling very confused. *Marie was coming on our weird writing trip too?* I loved my sister dearly, but Marie and peaceful environments didn't really go together. She was always loud and opinionated, and I had doubts about how much writing I'd be able to get done if she was there in Wales with us too. But on the other hand, the thought of staying in a remote cottage with Antoni had been freaking me out. So having my sister there might not be too bad after all. And maybe it would be a chance for us to have a good chat, to catch up on things, and for me to find out if she was okay, or if she was experiencing more problems than I knew about...

'It looks like Marie's coming to Wales with us too,' I said to Dad. 'She's just texted me about it.'

Dad looked at me and smiled.

'You know, Polly,' he said, 'I do think it's rather sweet that you two get on so well now. Given how much Marie used to dislike you when you were little.'

'Er, what?' I said. This was news to me. In my memories, Marie and I had always been close. But then I was aware that I tended to look at the past with rose-tinted glasses sometimes...

'Yes,' Dad went on, 'don't you remember? She was absolutely furious when you were born. Which was just natural jealousy towards a younger sibling, I suppose. Once, when you were in the baby bouncer, she piled cushions on top of your face when your mother had popped into the kitchen to make a tea. We always thought she was trying to do away with you that day.'

'Oh?' I said. 'No, I don't remember anything like that happening. But Marie's only two and a half years older than me, Dad. She would have still been tiny when she did that. I doubt she even remembers.'

'Ah yes,' Dad said. 'But her rage towards you came out every now and again for the next few years. Right up until you were both in primary school. And then she found a good group of friends, and calmed down. It really is great that the pair of you get on so well now. She's still got a temper on her though. She was here a few months ago, actually, and not in the best of moods for some reason.'

I smiled, trying to make light of what Dad had just told me. But a sense of disquiet had taken me over.

Chapter Twenty-One

The weekend was not the happy two days that it usually was when Danny and I were alone together. I felt stressed, trying to pack a travel bag with all the essentials that I'd need for a few days, while attempting not to let my worries filter through to my son. *What should I bring with me?* I wondered, distracted by the whole thing. *Phone charger, underwear, shampoo, laptop. What about food? Would we eat out every evening? I certainly couldn't afford to do that. Maybe we'd stop and get some essential bits on the way there?*

I presented the idea of Danny going to his grandad's for the following week as a great adventure, an opportunity for him to not only carry on exploring the 'jungle' outside, but also to find all the hidden nooks and crannies in the house. I regaled him with stories of when Marie and I were little, and how we used to play hide and seek – making Dad's house sound as exciting as humanly possible. My son was soon sold on the idea, and seemed absolutely fine about the prospect of spending a few days apart from me. Which was great, a weight off my mind. But I couldn't say I was feeling as calm as him about the whole thing.

Dad was old now, and not as mobile as he used to be. He'd

also started to forget the odd thing, like where he'd put something that he'd bought, or where he'd left his spectacles. *What if he forgot to pick Danny up from school one day?* I kept thinking. *What if he found it annoying, having a busy and boisterous little boy around for so long?* I knew that Dad loved his grandson very much, but it was one thing enjoying a child's company for the odd hour-long visit, and quite another keeping your patience with the same bouncy, active child for several consecutive days in a row, without any other adult to help take the pressure off you. I knew this all too well, from experience. And when I'd been young, Dad hadn't been as chilled as he now was. I could remember him shouting at Marie and I if we made too much noise when he was tired after a long day at work. Mum and Dad had quite a traditional sort of relationship; she'd been the caregiver, the compassionate one who'd cuddled us if we fell over, and he'd been the hard-working disciplinarian. Danny wasn't used to people shouting at him. Maybe I should have a word with Dad about it...

Christ, Polly, I gave myself a talking to while I hastily folded a pair of jeans and shoved them into my bag. *Stop being a helicopter parent. Give your son some room to breathe. He'll be fine. Dad will be fine. You'll be fine in Wales. Just relax. Stop being such an over-worrier.* An image of my mum, smiling at me, came into my mind. I'd be panicking about something or other, like the time when I was supposed to be going on a trip to Vienna as part of my university course, but I couldn't find my passport anywhere, despite turning the house upside down.

'Polly,' she'd said. 'You do get yourself in a state sometimes, don't you? Just remember, there's always a solution to every problem. Now, when did you last use your passport? Can you remember?'

Shortly after that, we'd found it in the side pocket of my suitcase. Me being my usual disorganised self hadn't even put it away from the last time I'd gone abroad. *Maybe I need to apply this kind of thinking to my current situation,* I told myself. *Going to Wales is just a solution to Sylvie's problem, that's all. And it's earning me some much needed pennies. I can just calm down, and everything will be all right.*

Will I be okay in Wales though? I immediately thought. *If it were a holiday with friends or family, then I'd be feeling much better about the whole thing.* But it was an enforced breakaway with a man I hated. Despised, even.

But you've committed to it, I told myself, ignoring the sinister feeling that was growing in my heart. *Just stop thinking about it and get on with it. You're doing this to help Sylvie get free from Antoni. You have to just write the book, and get it finished. How bad can it be, especially if Marie's there? And if you're being completely honest with yourself, you have so much to gain financially from this, Poll. And you fucking need these funds right now, for Danny's welfare, and for the future. So suck it up and get on with it. The whole thing will be over before you know it...*

Chapter Twenty-Two

I couldn't quite believe what was happening. How my steady little life had taken such a dramatic turn. It was Monday morning, and Marie, Sylvie, Antoni and I were hurtling down the M4 on our way to Wales. The sunshine that I'd been enjoying so much recently had been washed away by cold April rain. Marie was behind the wheel, her windscreen wipers ticking away, and I had to admit that her newish Land Rover Defender was much more comfortable to be in for a long ride than my Nissan Note or Sylvie's Ford Focus would have been. Despite their apparent money troubles, my sister and Henry always managed to drive top-of-the-range cars. Antoni – being the manipulator that he was – had recruited my sister so she could provide luxury travel for him. And seeing the three of them together, I was starting to understand that Marie actually got on much better with him than she did with Sylvie. Which was odd... She seemed much happier than she had been the other day at my house, in fact, she seemed elated, as though we were all going off on a jolly holiday together. As though she was completely blind to the fact that Sylvie and I had been forced – unwillingly – into complying with Antoni's egotistical dream of having this book written about him, as he was using it as leverage, saying it would be the key to getting him to leave Sylvie alone.

Sylvie and I were in the back; she was curled up in one corner looking like a skinny frightened animal. She'd barely said a word since I'd got in the car, although she had looked over and tried to give me a smile when I'd opened the door. I personally felt sick to the stomach that the monstrous man in the front passenger seat had managed to exert this much control over Sylvie, and now me. I had many misgivings about Antoni keeping his promise to fuck off and leave Sylvie alone once his bloody book was written, but I had to believe him. It seemed like the only chance she had to get her life back in order. To be free of him once again. And much as I'd rather not be there and be back at home with my son all week, I was glad that I could offer her this ray of hope.

Marie, on the other hand, hadn't stopped talking once, and I was wondering how on earth I was going to get this bloody book written with her around. I needed a quiet space to write in, and with my sister and Antoni cracking jokes and laughing loudly during the journey, this was looking like an increasingly doubtful prospect...

I was missing Danny already, and I hated the fact that I was being forced to spend five days away from him. Bringing him with me had been an unthinkable prospect, he needed to be kept safe. My son had been absolutely fine about it though, thrilled – in fact – to be going to spend so many days with Grandad. *Just think of the money, Polly,* I kept telling myself. *That's the only reason you're doing this. That's why you're here. And you'll be setting Sylvie free too. The time in Wales will pass really quickly, and you'll be back with Danny before you know it. Just get on with it, write the book quickly, and everything will be fine...*

Antoni had plotted out the route that he wanted us to take to Wales, and had apparently programmed Marie's satnav for her before they'd come to pick me up in Penge. *Of course he'd done this*, I thought. *He has to be in control of bloody everything.* It was irksome to me now when I saw one person being dominated by another in a relationship. Especially after everything that had happened just before I'd broken up with Jakub. It wasn't comparable with Sylvie's experiences, but still... *It's strange, Marie seems more than happy to fit in with his whims. I never thought she was like that...*

After we left the M4 at Newport in South Wales, we headed off onto a series of winding roads that led us deep into the Welsh countryside. Apparently we were heading for a place called Gartheli, and I'd phoned my dad to let him know as soon as Antoni had told me. Why we had to go so far away to write this book, I had no idea. But I'd learnt from Sylvie that there was no point in asking questions, because Antoni was in charge of everything and didn't like giving explanations for his whims. *He probably wanted a little holiday too*, I decided. *Spread his wings after being in prison for so long.* It looked like I was going to have to try and keep my independent thoughts to myself as much as possible while we were away on our little sojourn, if I wanted to keep the peace. Play along with Antoni's ego for a bit, just to get through the week as quickly as possible. *Maybe that's what Marie was doing, by pandering to all his requests?*

I willed the time in the car to go past as quick as possible. I just wanted to get the whole damn expedition over with as soon as we could. Marie and Antoni were getting increasingly noisy. The two of them seemed to get on really well, I noticed. Which was probably because Antoni was in a good mood, as everything was going his way and he was getting exactly what he wanted. Marie was acting as though they were best buddies. I just didn't understand it. It was like she'd chosen to completely ignore the fact that he was abusive. Controlling. Manipulative. *A criminal. Why would she do that?*

Two hours went by, and I became used to the grey-coloured cottages we were whizzing past, the bumpy roads, the increasingly high hills we were zooming up and down, and the glorious views that were beginning to unfold.

Wow, that's stunning, I thought, staring out over a beautiful panoramic vista that came into view as we reached the brow of another hill. It was like something from *Lord of the Rings. Strange that we are driving through such beauty when Sylvie and I are in such an ugly situation...*

We drove through another tiny village and onto a narrow road that was densely packed with trees on either side of it. At her satnav's signal, Marie did a hard right and screeched up a gravelly drive towards an old-looking largish cottage. As we approached the building, the front door opened, and two men walked out.

'Amigos,' Antoni called out of the window at them. 'You guys beat us to it.' He opened the door and jumped out of the car before Marie had finished grinding it to a halt. He ran over towards the two men.

I turned towards Sylvie.

'I thought it was just supposed to be us four staying here?' I said, panic rising up fast inside me. 'Who are they?'

Chapter Twenty-Three

Sylvie shook her head as she stared at the men.

'I'm so sorry, Polly,' she whispered. 'They're two of his gang friends. I had absolutely no idea that Antoni was inviting anyone else. He never tells me anything. Even if I'd known and tried to stop them from coming, he wouldn't have listened to anything I had to say about it. You know what he's like.'

I nodded, a sinking feeling in my stomach. Marie got out of the car and walked towards the group.

'Come on,' I said to Sylvie through gritted teeth. 'Let's get our bags and get this week over with, shall we?'

Right, Polly, I gave myself a talking to as I opened the boot of the car, *go inside, write the damn book, and keep looking forward to seeing Danny on Friday. You can look after Sylvie, and make sure that Antoni leaves her alone, when you're not interviewing him or writing. The days will fly by before you and Sylvie know it...*

I soon realised that Antoni's two friends – who'd arrived at the cottage before we had – were just as vile as him. Equally egotistical and inconsiderate. I had no idea what their real names were, but everyone referred to the one with the scar on his face as 'Stitches', and the shorter one with a mashed-up nose as 'Joe Bull'. These two men always called Antoni 'Axe Man'. Stitches was loud and vulgar, Joe Bull was more reticent and wore a permanent sneer on his face. They seemed to revere Antoni, who was clearly top dog amongst them.

'Pass me a glass,' Stitches had said to me when we were in the kitchen. Both his tone and his eyes had been hard. No please, no niceties. I'd pretended I hadn't heard him and turned away. Marie could pander to these arseholes if she wanted, but I certainly wasn't going to.

'Move,' Joe Bull had said to me in a commanding tone, when I'd had the audacity to walk across the hall when he was pulling a bag in through the front door. *Jesus*, I'd thought, slowing down a bit on purpose. *What a prick*. I almost came to a halt, a sense of injustice whooshing through me, one I hadn't felt for years. I was very close to telling the man to fuck off. It was on the edge of my tongue. But instead, I sauntered as slowly as I dared, listening to him mutter insults under his breath.

I was hating being in Wales already. Granted, Antoni had made an effort to give me a bedroom that was furthest away from the kitchen and living areas; it was up the stairs and right at the end of the corridor. He came into the bedroom with me, which made the hairs on the back of my arms stand on end. He pointed towards a plug socket.

'You can use that for your laptop, Polly,' he said. 'Plug it in. Now's the time for writing.'

As I stared at his eyes, I saw that unlike his lips – they weren't smiling.

'Sure,' I said. 'That's why we're here, isn't it? But before I can write anything, Antoni, I'm going to need to interview you again. I need the material about your life and exploits before I can start writing a manuscript that's all about you. I'm sure you have a really interesting tale to tell and I want to make sure that

I get every detail of it correct.' There, I did it. Lied to him and made it kind of seem like I wanted to tell his story. Because I knew that for there to be an actual chance that he'd leave Sylvie alone he had to like what I was writing. Acting like this made me feel sick though. I reached into my handbag and pulled out my Dictaphone. 'I need to record everything you say on this, so that I have all the material to hand – that I can rewind and fast-forward when necessary – when I sit down to turn what you both have said into an autobiographical account.'

Antoni glared at me. He clearly didn't like being told what to do even if it meant that it helped him reach his goal.

'Fine,' he said. 'Come back downstairs then, and we can get started.'

Ten minutes later, Antoni and I were sitting in the smaller living room – it turned out that there were two – the door firmly shut. I'd managed to give Dad and Danny a quick call before going down the stairs – on Dad's landline as he had always refused to get a mobile phone. It was lovely to hear their voices, but made me sad that I wasn't with them. Although it sounded like Danny was having a wonderful time, chicken Kyiv and chips for dinner and ice cream for dessert. From my seat in the living room, I could still hear Marie's voice – it penetrated through the walls from the kitchen where she, Stitches and Joe Bull had already started drinking vodka together. *Just block everything else out*, I told myself. *Just get this done, help Sylvie, go back home to Danny and forget that this weird trip away ever happened.*

'Right,' I said, turning on my Dictaphone. 'Let's get started. So, why don't you tell me a bit more – from your point of view – about what life was like in Poland when you were growing up. I bet you were popular and had loads of friends?'

God, he was a disgusting human being, I thought, as I listened to Antoni describing his teenage exploits, how he'd had girls hanging off him behind Sylvie's back, how he'd stolen from his neighbours without them ever realising. *Does he really think that people will admire him for all this?*

'Listen, Polly,' Antoni said, leaning forwards. I could see his giant tattooed muscles flex in his arms. 'Everything I learned in Poland helped me to get well up in the Palace City Boys when I moved to England. I want you to make that connection. There were only two other people above me in the end, in the gang. Together, the three of us fucking ran the whole of Crystal Palace. I was respected, when I went out everyone knew who I was.'

I nodded, trying not to let my real feelings show on my face.

'I see,' I said. 'That's fine. But I think we really need to concentrate on your time in Poland at the moment. Get things down in a chronological order, if you know what I mean.'

Antoni nodded and reached into his pocket, pulling out the burnt inhaler I'd seen him with in Sylvie's house, the end of which he then covered in tin foil – also from his pocket. He lit a cigarette, tapped the ash on top of the foil, and then put some sort of drugs on the ash. He lit it and inhaled deeply. Immediately that disgusting plasticky smell filled the room. I now knew for certain, after Sylvie confirmed it, that he was smoking crack. And he obviously felt comfortable enough with me, certain that I wouldn't go to the police, to do it in front of me. *How the hell,* I thought, *has my life come to this?* What made me most angry, I realised, was the fact that I was now scared of this bastard Antoni. I'd also trusted him – to some extent – after he'd left jail. I'd also bought into the fact that he was a changed man. And somehow he'd managed to manipulate a simple ghostwriting job into it being something I no longer had a choice in. It was the only way to free Sylvie from him, he said. He had a hold over me because of this, and he knew it. I had to finish this book, for Sylvie's safety. And probably for mine and Danny's too.

So over the next hour, I tried to put my heavy concerns out of my mind, and nodded along as – between smoking his crack pipe – Antoni arrogantly told me about his life.

At one point, the door handle turned and Marie came stumbling into the room. I could see how pissed she was at once, and I stared at her, wondering what the hell she was thinking, behaving like this. It reminded me of how she'd acted when she'd been about eighteen; always coming home drunk and having fights with our parents. But you expect that kind of thing from a teenager. Not so much from a forty-four-year-old mum. My feelings towards my sister had become very complex. Confused. I didn't understand her closeness to Antoni and her apparent lack of concern for Sylvie. And to be honest, I was hurt that she'd got me into such an unhealthy situation in the first place. She'd pretended that it was all for my benefit – to help me out financially – but had that really been her motivation? And when she'd got out of the car when we'd first arrived at the cottage, she greeted Joe Bull and Stitches as though she already knew them. What the hell was really going on here? I wanted to get her on her own, so I could question her about it all. But she was so hammered now that I doubted she'd make much sense. My chat with her would have to wait.

'Just come to see how you lovely people are getting on,' my sister slurred. 'Cheer up, Polly,' she said, taking a step towards me. 'Christ, you've got a face like a slapped arse. It's not that bad here, is it?'

'Hey, Marie?' a male voice called from the kitchen. 'Do you want some of this or not?'

Some of what? I thought, watching Marie turn round and stumble off out of the room. *Some more vodka? Something else? Drugs? Surely not...*

'Anyway,' Antoni said, trying to pull the attention back onto himself. He was up to the bit where Sylvie – willingly according to him – became an escort. 'I can remember Sylvie's first customer as though it was clear as day. It was a guy who answered our advert. He had a Polish name, but he was more of a Londoner than most cockneys I've met. Jakub. Jakub Wojcik.'

A strangled noise came out of my mouth and the Dictaphone rolled out of my fingers and onto the floor.

Chapter Twenty-Four

Jakub Wojcik was the name of my son's father. My ex-partner. The man who had phoned me the other day, demanding that I pay him some money. Could this be a coincidence? Perhaps there were two Jakub Wojciks in London? The room swam in front of me as I tried to get my head around what the actual fuck was going on...

The truth was that there was a large chunk of Jakub's life – the bit before he met me – that I didn't know about. We'd met in a jazz club one night, Pedro's in Greenwich. Brigitte and I had gone out for a few drinks, we both absolutely loved jazz music, and Pedro's was our favourite – and closest – haunt. I'd been single for just over a year at that point, my last relationship having been with a man called James, ending because he'd been transferred to New York by his company, and it turned out that neither of us felt strongly enough about each other to keep a transatlantic thing going.

Jakub had been by the bar with a couple of friends when we'd walked in, and he'd caught my eye immediately. He was laughing – a real belly laugh – at something one of his mates had just said, and this immediately attracted me to him. He seemed so genuine, and when he turned and saw me, his eyes stayed glued onto me for the rest of the night. We exchanged numbers, went out for some really fun dates, and soon became inseparable. I fell in love with Jakub fully and completely, and for a long time, I would have done absolutely anything for him. I thought I'd finally met the person who I'd spend the rest of my life with. And I do believe that he felt that way about me too. For a while, at least.

'He's so perfect,' I remember Jakub saying, as he bent down over our son's crib. 'Look at his little hands, Polly.'

'Yes,' I'd agreed. 'He's our beautiful boy, Jakub. We're so lucky.'

I was working on building up my writing career at the time, and it turned out that Jakub was a musician who was giving piano lessons to kids to earn some money. He also played the keyboard in a band, and was really good at what he did. We decided to move in with each other after a year or so, and we could only afford to rent a small studio flat, but we were more than happy up in the attic of an old Victorian townhouse. Danny came along a year after, and for a while everything was bliss.

But as funny and as genuine as Jakub was, he was also plagued by regular bouts of depression, and these affected his ability to work consistently. He'd have several months of getting along well, but then when his mood crashed he would end up cancelling several of his pupils' lessons in a row, causing the parents of these children to finally call it a day with him and go in search of a more reliable piano teacher. His dark moods also affected our relationship. Because although he was never horrible to me or anything, and always loved Danny very much, when he went into his mental cave he would withdraw from us, and deal with his thoughts and troubles internally. I often felt pushed out, although I tried my best to understand how he was feeling, and to give him the space and time that he needed in order to come up again.

Sometimes I would ask Jakub about what he thought caused these terrible bouts of depression, and he would vaguely allude to his hedonistic youth, and to the fact that he'd done things that he shouldn't have. He didn't want to go into more detail than this, but I presumed he meant alcohol and maybe drugs. Brigitte and I and our other small group of friends had lived life up at university, and although I always liked working I did let my hair down then and got drunk with everyone on a semi-regular basis. I knew how fun life was when you were young, and I often reassured Jakub that I wouldn't judge him if he told me a bit more about his past, but he never did. Maybe he thought I wouldn't understand.

Then one day, when he'd been going through a longer than usual bout of depression that was showing no signs of lifting, Danny and I came back from the park to find Jakub with a half empty bottle of vodka in his hand. He was asleep on the sofa. My heart sunk when I saw this, as he'd never drunk in the daytime by himself before, not that I knew of anyway. Over the next few weeks I encouraged Jakub to go to the doctor for help, to think about booking in some counselling sessions, to get more exercise. I even brought him some vitamins, thinking that they might give him a boost. But he resisted all of these suggestions, and just got drunk more and more often. It sometimes seemed that he actually liked living in a dark miasma of despair.

Soon, he spent more nights on the sofa, while me and Danny were in the bed. His behaviour towards me changed, although I never told anyone about this, I was too ashamed. I felt as though it was my fault, in some way. He could be so rude, putting me down and saying vile things. Although when he woke up the next day he rarely remembered what he'd done... It became clear to us both that our relationship had run its course, but it took ages for us to go our separate ways. I hated his drinking but I cared about him as a person. I'd felt like a single mother for ages by that point, as Jakub had been mentally slipping further and further away from Danny and I, and had stopped being an engaged partner or dad. Maybe that's why I'd become so independent since? Maybe this was a kind of protection for me, to not get attached to anyone else so that I didn't have to get hurt again?

Anyway, the truth of the matter was that I didn't know much about Jakub's former life. So if he'd been involved with Antoni at some point, did he already know something about me? It was a disturbing thought. Just how much was I in the dark about what was really going on here?

Chapter Twenty-Five

I shut myself in my room that evening, after having managed to scavenge two pieces of pizza from someone's plate in the kitchen. I'd checked on Sylvie, and she was curled up on her bed texting Filip. We'd chatted earlier, and had agreed that we both just wanted to stay out of everyone else's way as much as possible, and get the days over quickly.

I made another, longer phone call to Danny and my dad, although this was a bittersweet moment as it made me miss my son even more. After I'd finally said goodbye, my thoughts returned to the earlier conversation I'd had with Antoni.

'So,' I'd said, trying to sound casual, 'who was the guy Jakub that you mentioned?'

Antoni just smiled at me.

'Oh, just a friend who helped me out from time to time,' he'd said. *Damn, this wasn't helpful at all.* And however hard I tried to fish for information during the rest of the interview, Antoni didn't divulge anything more about his relationship with Jakub.

My life felt like it was fragmenting around me, and I could feel my head – my thoughts – starting to go. I now couldn't rely on most of the people who were in the cottage – not even my sister, as she just seemed to want to get drunk. And Sylvie was in such a fragile and damaged state. It felt like a terrifying predicament to be in. I'd decided to stick to my original plan, which was to get the book finished, so that I could actually make some decent money for once, and so that Sylvie and I could get out of there and away from the whole lot of them. Although – if I was completely honest with myself – I now knew I should have listened to my gut in the first place. This whole fucking escapade was clearly a big mistake. Probably the worst one I'd ever made...

Antoni and I had chatted for over two hours in the end, so I had a good amount of material to be getting on with. I fished my laptop out of my bag, plugged it in and placed it on the dressing table that was there, which was going to become my new writing desk for the remainder of the week.

I opened a new Word document – there was no point in carrying on with Sylvie's manuscript now – turned the Dictaphone on again, and listened as Antoni's arrogant tones filled the room. I began tapping away, intent on writing the piece to the best of my ability – and in a way that Antoni would be pleased with. Because I was working for him now. So that I could make some money, and so that Sylvie could be free. I became lost in the work, ignoring all the noises that sporadically floated up from the lower floor. The raucous laughing, the slamming doors, the pounding footsteps. I could smell crack in my bedroom now, all the men must be smoking it. It was a truly disgusting odour, and after this week – I decided – I never wanted to smell it again.

When I was over an hour into the latest recording, and had racked up seventeen hundred words on the new manuscript, I could no longer ignore the fact that nature was calling. I paused the Dictaphone, stood up, and opened my bedroom door, in search of a toilet.

It was at that point that another door opened and Antoni's friend, Stitches, followed by my sister, Marie, emerged. Stitches had no top on, and Marie was pulling on a jumper over her vest top. Behind them, I could see that the double bed was now unmade, with the duvet slumping down towards the carpet. It was more than obvious what they had just been doing. I stopped, trying to make sense of this scene. Stitches shot me a rueful grin, then galloped off down the stairs. Marie just stood there, the expression on her face unreadable.

'Marie,' I said, my words coming out slowly. 'What have you done?'

'Polly,' she said, the changing expressions on her face settling down into one of defiance. 'It's not what you think.' She was still drunk, her words were slurred together.

'Yes, yes it is,' I said, aware that tears were now falling from my eyes. 'It's exactly what I think.'

'Urgh,' Marie said, sounding annoyed. 'Listen, come with me. There's something that I need to explain to you.'

She took my hand and led me into the room, which turned out to be her allotted bedroom in the cottage.

'Now,' she said. 'Sit down on the bed, and just listen to what I have to say before you jump in with your moral objections. Okay?'

I sat down, but I didn't say anything. I just stared at my sister, tears still pouring down my cheeks. *Who actually was this woman in front of me?* She no longer seemed to be the Marie that I knew and loved. My sister felt like a stranger. My whole life had turned into a nightmare, and I wasn't exactly sure how this had happened so quickly and comprehensively.

Marie sat down next to me, and sighed.

'The money issues that Henry and I have been having are much worse than you know,' she said. 'They're really, really bad. Henry got in trouble at work a few months ago, apparently there's an investigation going on into a deal that he made, it seems that he may not have done things completely above board. His pay has been affected by this, and we're at the point of losing our house. Not to mention being unable to afford the children's school fees.'

'But I thought he was doing fine?' I said. 'You went to a work do with him the other day, Marie?'

She shook her head and then sighed again.

'No, Polly, I didn't go to a work do with him that night. I went to see a customer.'

'A what?' I said. I still couldn't quite grasp what she was trying to tell me. Maybe I didn't want to...

'Oh for goodness' sake,' Marie said, sounding exasperated. 'You still live in some childhood fantasy land, don't you, Poll. It's like your head is still up Enid Blyton's Faraway Tree or something. Look, real life isn't all unicorns and roses, you know. Sometimes you have to make tough decisions in order to survive. And that's what I had to do when our money started drying up.'

'What decision did you make?' I said, wiping my eyes.

'I get on with Antoni quite well,' Marie said. 'And one night I was telling him about my money issues. He said that he's started to get involved with his friend's escorting business, and asked if I wanted to work for him. At first I said no, but after I'd thought about it for a while and things with Henry hadn't improved, I said I'd give it a go. Antoni was really pushy about it actually, he didn't give me much of a choice in the end.' She looked down. 'It does make me feel ashamed, Polly. Which is probably why I've been drinking so much, to mask the pain.'

'Antoni's doing that again?' I said. I still couldn't digest what my sister was saying. 'Running an escort business?'

'Yep,' Marie said. 'He'll probably tell you about it when you guys come to that point in the book.'

'But what about Henry?' I said, grasping at thoughts as they floated through my stress-addled mind.

Marie snorted.

'Henry doesn't exactly know what I'm doing, he's just glad that I'm bringing home money at the moment,' she said. 'And to be honest, Polly, he's not that perfect either. There was one point about a year ago that I was sure he was seeing someone behind my back... It's not like he has any moral high ground to stand on with all of this. I'm just doing what I can to keep the children in their school, and to keep a roof over our head.'

'You think Henry might have had an affair?' I said. I was feeling weak now.

'Oh, Polly,' Marie said, exhaling. 'Like I said, you're such an innocent still. I haven't told you the more sordid details of my life because I didn't want to worry you. You're like Pollyanna or Anne of Green Gables. You've got the right name for it – I'll give you that. A wholesome young gal who needs to believe that everyone is all right all the time.'

'Am I?' I whispered.

Marie nodded.

'Look,' she said. 'Obviously don't say anything about what I'm doing to Dad, okay? He's not in the best of health, and I don't want to make him feel any worse. I'm just doing this until we are in a better place financially. It's business. I'm offering a service, that's all. You really don't need to worry, all right?' She leaned over and grabbed a wad of notes from her dressing table. 'And see, I just had a quick bonk with Stitches and earned myself sixty quid. It's so easy. I have to give ten of it to Antoni, but I keep the rest.'

I stared at my sister. I could no longer take any of this in. The introvert side of me needed to crawl under a duvet and let the thoughts in my mind keep swimming until they reached some sort of sense.

I nodded, and then stood up.

'Okay,' I said, sniffing. I didn't want to look at Marie anymore. 'If you're sure you're happy with it.' I made to leave the room.

'Remember,' Marie called after me. 'Don't tell Dad.'

My head shot round.

'As if I would.' My words came out like gunfire.

As I walked back into my room and shut my door, immediately crawling under the duvet, the tears came back in full force. I buried my head in the pillow, and let the racking sobs overtake me. My sister was prostituting herself. And I'd had no idea. Oh my God. Maybe she was right, maybe I was just a simple, innocent Pollyanna person who had no idea what was really going on in life. Everything had changed now.

Chapter Twenty-Six

When I went downstairs to find some sort of breakfast the next morning – Tuesday – I could feel that something inside me had changed. It was like this heavy weight had arrived in my head and heart, and it showed no signs of shifting. I wasn't Pollyanna anymore, I was in survival mode.

My plan was to get some water, find something to eat – luckily Stitches and Joe Bull had had the sense to bring bags of food with them, probably on Antoni's orders – so there were loads of crisps and chocolate, as well as microwave burgers and chips in the fridge. Not really my sort of thing, but I was starving, and if I was going to carry on with the book I'd need something in my stomach. I found a glass, filled it to the brim, picked up a packet of ready salted crisps, and walked out of the kitchen with them towards the staircase. I hadn't been able to carry on with the typing last night, not after what Marie had told me. I'd been too distraught, and had ended up crying myself to sleep. I needed to get the latest recording written up quickly so that I could interview Antoni again in a few hours.

I heard light footsteps coming down the stairs, and then Sylvie's head appeared at the door.

'I'm going for a walk,' she said with a small smile. 'The more I stay away from Antoni and those men the better. Will you be all right here, Polly?'

'Yes.' I nodded. 'I did a lot of writing last night, and I want to get cracking with more today. Enjoy your walk.'

I had no idea how long everyone else had stayed up last night, but the cottage was already a tip. The kitchen was covered in overflowing ashtrays and empty vodka and beer bottles, and the stench of crack still hung in the air. I didn't actually think that anyone else – other than Sylvie – was up. I thought they'd be sleeping – passed out – in their rooms for a good few hours yet. But as I reached the first step, I heard low murmured voices coming from the larger of the two living rooms.

My first instinct was to go and listen to whoever it was talking, but without making myself heard. I wanted to gather as much information about what was going on as I could. Forewarned is forearmed, as they say, I thought. I inched towards the room, trying not to make a sound.

'Yeah, like I told you, Axe Man, it's a bit of a predicament,' a male voice said. Either Stitches or Joe Bull. 'A lesson is going to have to be learned here, if you know what I'm saying. The boy's done wrong.'

'Leave it with me,' Antoni's voice said. 'I'll sort it, okay?'

'I'll come with you,' another male voice said. It sounded like Stitches that time. 'It could get really fucking nasty. There might be more of them around, if you know what I mean.'

'No,' Antoni said, as commanding and arrogant as ever. 'I'll go by myself. You two stay here. You need to keep an eye on things. Make sure that writer keeps going with the book. She writes bestsellers and she's doing one for me. She's my ticket to the big time, boys. No one else goes anywhere while I'm gone, okay?'

'Yes, boss,' one of the other two said.

I crept back towards the stairs, and then up into my room. So Antoni was going somewhere? I mean, on the one hand that was good news as I couldn't stand the man. But on the other it wasn't at all great as I wanted to get the bloody book finished ASAP, and if he wasn't around it meant that I couldn't interview him. Oh well, nothing I could do about that. He did seem rather deluded about how famous this frigging manuscript was going to make him, but who was I to take his dreams away? And it was a bit odd that he was just going to leave, wasn't it? After all the effort of getting us all to Wales? If he thought that I was going to work on the book for a day longer than Friday then he was sorely mistaken...

Footsteps pounded up the stairs.

'Marie?' Antoni's voice called. 'I need to use your car. Give me your keys, will you?'

There was no answer. I wasn't surprised. My sister had been so out of it the evening before that she was probably dead to the world.

'Marie?' Antoni said, louder this time. 'Give me your car keys.' For a moment, anxiety tugged at my heartstrings. *Was my sister okay? I should be keeping a closer eye on her...*

'They're on my dresser,' a muffled voice called back. *Phew.*

There was the sound of a door opening, footsteps, clinking of keys, then the door shutting again. I heard Antoni go into another room. It sounded like he was dragging something heavy across the floor, or out of a cupboard. A few minutes later, he'd gone back downstairs and I heard the front door slam. The car revved into life, and he drove away. We were free from him. For a while, at least...

Chapter Twenty Seven

The next few hours passed relatively peacefully. I worked hard at the book, making the best of Antoni's words, and writing it in a way that I hoped he'd like. I could hear Stitches and Joe Bull downstairs, and from the smell of it they'd already started their morning crack pipes. My sister didn't wake up until after midday, at which point I heard her bedroom door open, and her walking slowly to the bathroom. I felt sad that we were clearly not as close as I'd always thought we were. She was making life choices that I thought would be disastrous for her and her family in the long run, and she was acting like a rebellious teenager while we were in Wales. *I'm just doing this so Sylvie can be free*, I thought. *And so that I can get my normal life back.* In three days, come Friday, Antoni would leave Sylvie alone – if he kept his word – and I'd be going home, and that's all I cared about... *Although,* my treacherous brain then said, *after everything you now know, Polly, do you think that Antoni will really keep his word? That you'll get your money and that Sylvie will be set free from his clutches?* I shook my head. The implications of these thoughts were too dire to digest... I had to believe he would keep his promises. Because otherwise...

By 2pm, I'd finished using up the last bit of the most recent recording. I closed my laptop, and suddenly realised how starving I was again. I didn't really want to see any of the others, but at the same time I needed some food. So I made my way downstairs and into the kitchen, retrieving a disgusting-looking burger in a plastic wrapper from the fridge, and placing it in the microwave.

The heavy feeling in my head and heart was still there, weighing me down. It was as though a veil had been drawn away from my eyes and I was seeing the darkness in my world for the first time. I'd always been interested in true crime, and had read countless books and watched numerous TV programmes about it. But I'd previously had a sense that that sort of thing belonged to another place that I wasn't a part of, another universe even. But now, I could see that the darkness surrounded me too. Maybe it always had. It wasn't just Antoni and the rest of them that I was including in this, it was the hate, the fear, the disgust and the crime that I now felt implanted in. I mean, Christ, I'd always lived in South London, hadn't I? It wasn't as though crimes hadn't gone on around me throughout my life. There had been the regular headlines of knife attacks, burglaries and even the odd murder in the local paper. But I'd always felt like I was in a bubble. Yes, maybe a Pollyanna bubble, where that sort of thing couldn't and wouldn't touch me.

But now it had. The bubble had burst. I could see now that everyone had darkness in them as well as light. Even me, probably. I should have been more responsible. Not had my head buried in the clouds quite so much. Not been so reliant and co-dependent on other people. And Marie? Well. As Dad had so recently pointed out, she'd hated me when we were little; a fact I'd so conveniently chosen to forget. And now she was doing what she needed to in order to survive. Maybe I would make the same choice as her if I was ever put in that position, where I was actually going to lose my house and take my child out of school? No, I shook my head. I don't think I would. I'd rather home-school Danny and live in a tent than sell my body.

'Oh, Polly, there you are,' Sylvie said, coming in. 'I just got back from my walk. How's the book going?'

'Fine,' I said, pleased to see her. I gave her a small smile. 'I'm all up to date with it, I've managed to get loads done. Although we need to keep up the pace, so I could do with sitting down for another interview with Antoni as soon as possible.'

'Ah,' Sylvie said, pulling a face. 'I'm not sure if that's going to be possible actually, Polly. He's been called away on some sort of business or other. At least that's what he said in his message. God knows what he's really up to.'

'Oh I see,' I said. 'Yes, I heard him saying he needed to go out earlier. He asked my sister for her car keys. I was hoping he might be back soon. It's just that we've only got until Friday to finish this book, haven't we? And then we're all going home, and I'm really missing Danny so I'd like to keep to the time frame. We're going to need to work as hard as possible to get the manuscript finished by then.'

'Hmm,' Sylvie said, her brow creasing. Then she turned her eyes onto me and I saw the anxiety in them. 'Antoni texted me again a couple of hours ago. He thinks we might all have to stay here a bit longer than Friday, Polly. I'm so, so sorry, but you might have to tell whoever is looking after Danny to hang on to him for a few more days...'

Chapter Twenty-Eight

There is no way, I thought, stomping back up the stairs with my revolting burger, *that I am staying in this shit pit a day longer than Friday*. There was no point in talking to Sylvie about this, it wasn't her fault that Antoni had gone somewhere, and all she'd done was pass on his message. She had as little control as me over the man and his whims. I'd agreed to do this in order to help her, and I was glad that I had, but at the same time I most definitely wanted to be back in South London with my son by Friday evening. And I was going to tell Antoni that, whenever he came back from selling people crack or whatever he was up to...

I decided that I'd have to eat the rank burger, despite my misgivings. It was either that or starve. But first I needed the toilet. I opened my door and saw Joe Bull walking across the landing.

'By the way,' I said to him. 'You can tell Antoni that I won't be staying here in Wales any longer than Friday. I need to get back to my son then. I just wanted to make that clear. Okay?'

Joe Bull stopped and slowly turned his ugly face towards mine.

'You,' he said, taking a step towards me, 'will do as you're fucking told, my girl. And if the boss tells you to stay here for another week, then that's what you're going to do. Especially if you want to see your little boy all happy and healthy when you get home. You understand?'

I couldn't talk. Fear was gripping me now. Was this man actually threatening me? With the safety of Danny? What the actual fuck?

I retreated back into my room, closing the door with my shaking hand. The toilet would have to wait. Things had taken a turn for the worse. I was now a prisoner, being kept here against my will. I'd been threatened by Joe Bull. And while I was scared, I was now also really fucking angry. No one put my son in danger. Things had gone too far now. Action was needed; and I had to think about the best way to get myself – and Sylvie and Marie – out of here. Not that my sister would go willingly, but still. Maybe if I explained what was happening to her when she was sober she would understand...

I glanced at my phone, and saw that it was only 4pm. Right, I'd promised to stay in Wales till Friday, but if I could I would make an escape before that... I'd hated being there even before Joe Bull had said what he did, and I could tell that Sylvie felt the same – she was looking more and more stressed by the day. I had to be with Danny; his safety had been threatened and that was too much.

Things were hotting up downstairs once more. Marie must be on the vodka again because she was sounding decidedly more animated than when she'd woken up. There was no way I'd be able to talk to her now, and explain why we had to get the fuck out of Wales.

I sat back on my bed and thought hard...

Chapter Twenty-Nine

The screeching tyres on the gravel outside jolted me into consciousness. For a minute I had no idea where I was. *Had I overslept? Was Danny now late for school?* Oh fuck. The realisation that I was somewhere in Wales slammed into me like an out of control articulated lorry. Tears sprang to my eyes and I wiped them away furiously. No, I wasn't going to get upset. I was going to get up, go downstairs, make sure Sylvie was all right, interview Antoni and get on with the book. And put my plan into action. I had to speak to Sylvie and Marie, they had to understand how important it was that we get away from these men as soon as possible. And I was feeling stronger now than I had for years. *Nothing like a bit of seething anger to make your feistiness return...*

I leaned over and grabbed my phone from the bedside table. It was 10.47am on Wednesday. Ten minutes later, I was up, washed, dressed and trotting down the stairs. Antoni was standing in the hall talking to Joe Bull and Stitches in a low voice. I stopped and stared at him for a moment, surprised by his appearance. He looked terrible. He had a cut lip, dried blood upon his face, dirt everywhere, and tears in his jeans and top. *What the...?*

'Antoni,' I said, trying to sound businesslike. No matter what he'd done, or why he looked the way he did, we had important stuff to be getting on with. 'Nice to see you. Have you seen Sylvie yet this morning?'

'She's gone for a walk,' Stitches said. Antoni just turned and glared at me.

'Great,' I said. 'Er, Antoni, would it be okay if we cracked on with another interview in a few minutes? It's just that we only have two more days after today to get the book done, so we really need to get on with it.'

'No,' he said. Walking down the remaining steps, I saw that both his eyes were red and swollen. One of them was filled with blood. 'Now's not a good time. We'll have to stay in Wales a bit longer. There's some stuff I need to attend to today.'

'I'm not staying here longer than Friday.' The words came out of my mouth quickly. 'I can't do that, Antoni. I need to get home. Sylvie needs to get back too, and I'm sure Marie does as well. We all have children who need us to be around at the weekend. We had an arrangement; let's stick to it.'

'We'll stay here as long as we need to, Polly,' he said, his voice loud now. 'Make the necessary arrangements.' His expression was so aggressive, a shiver of fear rushed through me. But I was angry too. I thought of Danny...

'No, I can't do that I'm afraid,' I said, feeling the hot anger run through my veins again. 'I need to get back to my son.'

'Ah yes,' Antoni said, walking towards the stairs. 'How is young Danny doing, Polly? Where's he staying at? Oh yes, I remember.' He rattled off my dad's address, word for word. He even got the postcode right.

I stared at him, ice-cold fear overtaking the fury.

'Let's have no more problems,' Antoni said. 'We're finished

with the book when I say we are, okay? Until then, just enjoy this nice little trip we're all on together, Polly. And stop whinging. Now go away. There's things I need to do.'

'Do not,' I said loudly, my words coming out slowly, 'ever talk to me like that again, Antoni. And if you threaten me or my son one more time then this book deal is off. Do you understand me?'

Chapter Thirty

I lay on my bed, staring at the ceiling. I'd always known that I loved Danny fully and unconditionally, but now that I was having this enforced separation from him I was realising the true depth of that love. Being apart from him had seemed just about bearable when I had Friday to look forward to; it was an achievable goal, the end of the working week, it had been the day when we would be reunited. But now Antoni was trying to throw away that goal. And my inner protective tiger instincts were in full flow as a result. I was fully focused on my escape from Wales, and intent on bringing Sylvie and Marie with me. Antoni hadn't liked me answering back to him, his face had been a picture of confusion and rage. But he needed me, and that was leverage. He and I were now in a delicate mental war, one where we both had some sort of control over the other. He knew he needed me for his stupid book. Fuck him, and the bloody manuscript. All I needed to do now was talk to the other women and get them onside with my plans to leave as early as possible but Sylvie was still out and Marie was no doubt hung-over...

Why had I been so stupid and agreed to come to Wales? My

mind was reeling. For all my new-found bravado, I was wondering what Antoni would do to me once I'd finished the book. Would he let my life with my son continue peacefully? He hadn't been a man of his word so far. What if he hated what I'd written? What if he wanted me to write a whole other book? What if he thought I knew too much about his life and wanted to do away with me? *Stop, Polly,* I told myself. *Just stop this. You're losing your shit now. And Danny needs you to stay strong. Take some deep breaths and calm down.*

I decided to go downstairs and be with the others. Try and find a way to speak to Marie privately, and then Sylvie whenever she returned.

I went to the upstairs bathroom on the way, but there was someone else in there. I heard Sylvie speaking in a low voice on the phone; she'd clearly got back from her walk while I was in my room. Good. I'd come back up and have a word with her in a few minutes. I went downstairs to the ground-floor toilet, and pushed open the door. Antoni was in there, soaking some clothes in the sink. He swung round.

'Fuck off,' he said, reaching over to slam the door in my face.

I was desperate, so I decided to go in the overgrown cottage garden instead. Then I walked back into the house, deciding to go to the larger of the two living rooms, where I could hear a TV playing.

'Hi,' I said, walking in, quickly scanning the room. Marie was on the sofa, staring at the TV. She raised her hand in a wave, then patted the cushion next to her. I walked over and sat down. Despite our recent problems, she was still family, and I wanted to help her with whatever she was going through somehow. Joe Bull and Stitches were also in there, their eyes trained onto the screen.

What's so captivating that everyone is sucked into it? I

wondered, turning towards the TV myself. It was the BBC News.

'The axe attack took place on the Oakhill Estate in Colliers Wood last night,' a young reporter was saying to the camera. 'One man was pronounced dead at the scene, and another is critically ill in hospital. Police are appealing for witnesses, although so far no one has come forward...'

I held my breath. *Colliers Wood?* That was where the rival gang to the Palace City Boys reigned. The enemies of Antoni, and – as I now knew – Stitches and Joe Bull. I turned my head and looked at the two men sitting near me. I watched as Joe Bull leaned over and murmured something to Stitches, who then nodded. And I knew, just knew, from their facial expressions, that Antoni had been involved in the axe attack that the BBC were reporting. Their thousand yard stares gave them away, their tense body language. They might be hardmen, but clearly the seriousness of murder still penetrated their iron emotions. And his gang name was Axe Man, wasn't it? So he hadn't been out dealing, as I'd presumed. He'd been out murdering. Killing. And I knew this. I had information that the police needed. But Antoni and Joe Bull were already threatening my son and I, about a bloody book. My life would definitely be in danger if he ever thought I was considering telling the police what I now suspected he'd done...

The TV camera panned round to a tear-stained older woman.

'Harvey Grant's mother is here with me now,' the reporter was saying. 'How are you feeling, Elaine, knowing that your son's killer is still on the loose?'

The woman sobbed.

'I just want to know who did this to my son,' she managed. 'Who would want to kill a seventeen-year-old? Harvey has always been such a good boy. He never hurt anyone. Please, if anyone knows anything, I beg you to tell the police today.'

The reporter turned back to the face the camera.

'If you have any information about this heinous crime and would like to get in touch with Metropolitan Police, please call the number that you can now see at the bottom of your screens...'

I now had information that could help the police to solve a crime. But if I told them what I knew, my life would no doubt be as good as over. And I needed – so desperately – to get Marie, Sylvie and I away from this house.

Chapter Thirty One

Back upstairs, I lay down on my bed and shut my eyes. It sounded like the TV had been switched off now, and music turned on. The alcohol must be flowing once again, as I could hear Marie's piercing laugh coming up through the floorboards. I was worried about her now. Especially in light of everything I now knew about Antoni and his so-called friends. I hoped she was managing to keep herself safe, in whatever way was necessary. I had to believe that she would. I knew she wouldn't listen to me if I went down and suggested she had an early night or anything. They would all just laugh and drink more. Stitches was getting noisy too. I turned over, I didn't even want to think about what the two of them might get up to in a bit...

How could I even start to process what I now suspected Antoni had done to that boy, Harvey Grant? I thought. Things had just gone to a whole new level of horrific. Smoking crack, dealing drugs and generally treating Sylvie and everyone else like shit was one thing. But murdering someone? Theoretically I could be wrong about Antoni's involvement in this crime, but in my bones I knew he'd had something to do with it. I couldn't forget the faces of his accomplices as they'd stared at the screen, the way Joe Bull had leaned over to his friend and whispered something, and the way Stitches had nodded. But was there anything I could do with my suspicions? Anyone I could tell?

I turned over the other way. It was as though the information and horror in me wouldn't let me lie still. Could I talk to Sylvie about this? I wondered. Yes, I could. It's exactly what I needed to do. She already knew what Antoni was capable of; he'd attempted to kill her once, for God's sake. She would understand more than anyone about this.

A large part of me felt compelled to phone the police right then and there. *I could be quiet about it, I could whisper what I knew to the emergency services operator. Maybe they'd send the police out at once, and he'd get locked up? Perhaps there would still be trace evidence on his washed clothes? But then,* I thought, *maybe there wouldn't.* All I had to go on were the reactions of Stitches and Joe Bull when the BBC News was on, my gut feeling, and the circumstantial evidence of Antoni being away from the house at the time of the crime. It wasn't enough to get him on at all, and in my heart I knew that. And I also had a good idea about what Antoni would do to me when he found out that I'd reported him. I'd never see my son again. Because I'd be chopped up by Axe Man.

I crept out of my room, knocked on Sylvie's door, and then pushed it open. She was lying on her bed, her gaunt face white.

'Oh hi, Polly,' she said, sitting up.

'Sylvie.' I sat down next to her. 'Listen, things have got really serious.'

I explained everything to her, about Joe Bull and Antoni's threats to me and Danny, about how I suspected him of killing Harvey Grant and the reasons for this.

'We're not safe here,' I said. I was talking so quietly hardly any sound was coming out. 'You, me and Marie need to get out of here as quickly as we can.'

Sylvie stared at me for a moment and then nodded.

'You're right,' she said softly. 'All of us are in danger while we're near Antoni, Polly. But think of what he would do to us if we left this house before Friday. If you think we aren't safe now, it's nothing compared to what we would be if we left Wales early without his permission. He's a fucking lunatic. And he's convinced that this book you're writing is going to be his ticket to success, and that it will immortalise him forever. He's obsessed with getting it done. Please, can we just stay until Friday afternoon? I'll talk to him, tell him you have to get back then and that you can't stay any longer, okay? But please just hang on here for as long as we agreed.'

I stared at her, my mouth open.

'It's my only chance to break free of him, Polly,' she said, tears in her eyes now. 'He promised he would let me go once you'd finished the book.'

'And do you think he'll keep that promise?' I said. My words sounded aggressive. 'After everything he's already done?'

Sylvie shook her head.

'I don't know,' she said. 'But please, help me to find out? If we sneak away now, Antoni will kill me for sure. And Filip needs me, Polly. I'm so, so sorry you've become involved with all this, you don't deserve any of it. But I'm asking you from the bottom of my heart to please stay here until the end of Friday?'

Chapter Thirty-Two

It was 8am on Thursday. Antoni had just barged into my room, woken me up, and told me to come downstairs to start the next interview with him for the book. I'd slept in fits and starts and felt ill with exhaustion.

'You've got ten minutes,' he'd said as he'd shut the door loudly.

It had taken me hours to get to sleep in the first place last night, after I'd spoken to Dad and Danny – trying my best to sound normal for them so that they wouldn't worry. I was pissed off that Sylvie had made me promise to stay until Friday. I understood her fear, how she still believed that Antoni might let her go if I kept to my end of the bargain, but keeping Danny's life safe – and my own – was of the utmost importance. I'd have to see how things went over the next few hours. If anything else bad happened, I was out of there, and I'd try my best to take my sister with me...

At least we now have a chance at getting this book finished, I thought as I dressed myself. *If I write quick enough we might still be able to get it done before tomorrow evening.*

I was washed, dressed and downstairs within eight and a

half minutes. I found Antoni lounging on the sofa in the smaller living room. Clearly this had become our designated interview space.

'So,' I said as brightly as I could. 'Let's get started. Why don't you pick up where you left off before, Antoni?' *I'm in a room with a murderer*, I thought.

He was looking a lot better than he had been yesterday, I thought, watching him scratch his stubbly chin as he tried to remember the last thing that he'd told me. He'd cleaned up his face and most of the swelling had gone down, although his right eye was still bloodshot.

He soon got into a flow, a continual boasting about his life and criminal conquests. How successful Sylvie was as an escort, how many customers she saw in a week, the expensive cars he was able to buy, the jewellery, the bling, the clothes – all designer brands of course. Then he told me about the attack on him and Sylvie, and how she'd lost the baby after it. How he was amazing, fearless, respected – possibly the best gangster of all time. Definitely since the Krays. How members of the Colliers Wood Gang jumped them one night as they were making their way back to their apartment. He didn't seem at all sad about the miscarriage though, just pissed off that he'd been disrespected and attacked.

'So obviously there were reprisals,' he said. 'In the weeks after that.'

I nodded. I wasn't going to ask any questions about these, the less I knew about his criminal life the better. I already knew too much.

'You've got enough there to be getting on with, Polly,' Antoni said, standing up. His eyes were hard. 'You can spend the rest of the day writing. I have things I need to do now.'

So that was that, interview over. On Antoni's command, as always.

As I made my way back up to my room, a small glimmer of hope started to shine in my brain. *If I work hard and write all this material up today,* I thought, *then maybe we will still have time to finish the rest of the book before tomorrow afternoon. And maybe, just maybe, Sylvie and I will be able to go back to South London on Friday without Antoni making any sort of objection. But if he does, what then? How far would I be prepared to go in order to keep Danny safe, get back to him? Would I steal the car? Would I actually be able to hurt someone if they stood in my way?* I knew at that point, with the inner protective tigress rising up in me, that I'd do whatever was necessary to get to Danny...

Chapter Thirty Three

By late afternoon, after working hard on the manuscript all day, trying to throw the infamous light on Antoni and his exploits that I knew he wanted, I was hungry. And I needed to check on Sylvie, see that she was okay. I didn't want to see anyone else though, so I decided to open my bedroom door as quietly as possible and creep down the stairs, find some food, and then go back to my room to do more work.

The first part of my plan went well, and I was soon down in the hall, getting my bearings for a minute. The whole place was strangely quiet. Maybe Sylvie had gone out for one of her walks; I knew that she liked to be as far away from Antoni as possible at all times. The others had probably tired themselves out last night, and were still sleeping.

But then as I made my way towards the kitchen, I heard some low voices. I stopped and listened...

'Yeah, it was a fucking mess,' I heard Antoni say. 'I couldn't get it done as quickly as I wanted, there were other people there too. They jumped me as soon as I started on Harvey.'

Oh fuck, I thought. This was proof that Antoni *had* killed the boy. I'd heard it with my own ears, he'd just admitted to it. I was now a witness, not just someone who suspected him on a hunch. I couldn't walk, I was rooted to the spot. If Antoni knew that I'd overheard him, bad things would *definitely* happen to me and maybe to Danny and my dad. I needed to get away from the hall, in case he came out. But I couldn't move...

I heard someone – Stitches or Joe Bull – mumble something in reply.

Go now, Polly, I told myself. *You have to get out of here. Move your legs...*

Very, very carefully, I lifted one foot and placed it in the direction of the kitchen. Good, my step hadn't made a sound. Now for another, then another.

Creak...

Fuck, some old floorboard below the carpet had just made a noise.

As the low voices stopped, and I heard footsteps, then a door opening, I flung myself forwards and into the kitchen, quickly grabbing the kettle and filling it up with water.

Antoni appeared at the door.

'I didn't know anyone was down here,' he said. His eyes were hard, boring into me.

'Oh hi,' I said. But it came out all wrong. Squeaky and unnatural. 'Yeah, I'm just making a cup of tea. Parched. Been working so hard upstairs for ages. Do you want one?'

He shook his head, still staring at me. Obviously trying to work out if I'd heard what he'd been talking about.

'Er, where's Sylvie?' I said, my words coming out too quickly. 'I thought she might like a drink too.'

'Gone for a walk,' Antoni said. 'Marie's still asleep, Stitches says.' Then he turned and walked away.

Fuck, I thought, realising that my hand – that was holding the kettle – was shaking. *Antoni wasn't stupid. He would now know – or strongly suspect – that I'd heard him talking about Harvey. And he'd know that the murder had been covered by the media – Stitches and Joe Bull would have told him that they saw it, that we were all watching it together.*

What was he going to do now?

Chapter Thirty-Four

It was Friday morning, and my fear was turning to paranoia. Antoni had come and opened my door last night when I was trying to work, and had just stared at me for ages. Probably trying to intimidate me, letting me know that he knew that I knew what he'd done. I'd tried, and failed, to remain looking as calm as possible. I wanted to convince him – without actually saying anything – that I hadn't heard a thing. But it was impossible. We both knew what had happened. That I'd heard him talking about Harvey. And only time would tell what he was planning to do about this...

I hadn't slept a wink, constantly on guard in case Antoni came into my bedroom again. My thoughts had gone out of control, I was imagining all sorts of wildly awful things happening. I'd made myself type away furiously the evening before, abject terror driving me on to finish the book, and had managed to write up the whole of the recording of Antoni's interview. It was entirely unlikely that Antoni would now just leave Sylvie and I alone with this new horrific turn of events, but I had to hope. Had to get us into the best position possible, just in case.

The index finger on my right hand was numb – clearly it was the one I used most when typing – and I had a cracking headache that felt like a vice was clamped on both sides of my forehead. My breathing was shallow, my heart rate hammering, and sweat was permanently on my body. We were so close to finishing the manuscript now, but then this had happened, and I didn't know what – if anything – Antoni was planning to do about it. For all he knew, maybe I didn't hear anything about what he was saying about Harvey. But then he'd heard my footstep, and he would have guessed. But he didn't have any actual proof, just suspicions. I wished I was a better actor, had been able to style the whole thing out more successfully, but fear had got the better of me. It had all happened so fast. Been so unexpected. *Stay strong, Polly. You can get through this, one way or another...* I felt a surge of hatred for Antoni go through me, and I was glad, because anger came with it. My new-found strength was returning. *Fuck this shit*, I thought. *I'm going to sort it out. Get this book done, and get out of this hellhole...*

I went in search of Antoni. It was the only thing to do; demand that we finish the manuscript. If I could just pin him down to another interview then it was entirely feasible that I could have the whole thing typed up by early afternoon if I really pushed myself. It would be done and dusted. Sylvie would be a free woman, and so would I. If Antoni allowed it...

'Hi, Stitches,' I said, walking into the larger living room. 'Have you seen Antoni anywhere?'

'He's gone out,' Stitches said. 'Got business.' He glared at me. No doubt Antoni had told him about me probably overhearing what they'd been discussing the day before. *Shit.*

I went cold. No, no, not again. If Antoni had gone somewhere again – to what, attack yet another person? To get more weapons? – then he would definitely try and delay our time in Wales. And it meant that he had the car, so I wouldn't be able to put my escape plan into action quite so easily should I want to. Perhaps he was doing this on purpose, it might be all part of his plan to punish me for being downstairs in the wrong place yesterday...

'Oh,' I said. It felt like my jaw was locking. 'I need to interview him for the book.'

'Axe Man said we'll be here till Monday at the earliest,' Stitches said. 'So get used to it.'

At which point I lost it.

Tears came pouring down my cheeks. The one hope that I'd been clinging to, that if I worked hard and fast enough then we could still go home on Friday evening, was dashed to pieces. I was a witness to the aftermath of a murder, and Antoni knew it. I was emotionally destroyed from missing my son and now I was embroiled in a horror that was only just beginning. And Antoni had the fucking car...

A wailing sound filled my ears, and I realised that it was me making it. I couldn't stop. I sat down on the carpet and leant against the wall. Stitches looked away.

'I want to see Danny,' I kept saying, over and over again. 'I want to see Danny.'

'Polly?' It was Marie making her way down the stairs, very bleary-eyed. 'What's wrong, babe?'

I tried to explain, but I was finding it hard to talk through my sobs. I couldn't tell her about what Antoni had done to Harvey; that would be like signing my own death warrant. I couldn't tell anyone, not even Sylvie. I had to live through this nightmare by myself...

'Oh no, that's absolutely ridiculous,' Marie said once she'd finally understood what I was telling her. She was sounding more like her old self. 'I have to get back to Beckenham today, Oliver's in an archery competition tomorrow and I promised him I'd be back in time to watch it. Not that we'll be able to afford to send him to those classes for much longer. Where's Antoni? I'll go and talk to him about this now.'

'Gone out on business,' Stitches told her.

'Well, when's he coming back?' Marie was annoyed now. It was like she was returning to being her usual self, after a hedonistic, anarchic personality holiday.

'Later,' Stitches said.

'Today?' Marie said.

'Yep,' Stitches said.

'Right, well can you phone him and ask him to hurry up, please?' Marie said. 'We'll need to get going by five at the latest, if we want to have a chance of getting into our own beds at home before midnight. Come on, Polly, let's go and get you cleaned up. You're a mess, which isn't surprising really, given how hard you've been working all week.'

I stood up and followed my sister up the stairs, feeling like I was having an out-of-body experience. On some level, I was aware that my sister's persona had flipped back to how it usually was. *Maybe she just needed to blow off some steam due to all the stress she's been under? Maybe she's just been going through some sort of horrendous blip? God, I hope so. Maybe she'll stop prostituting herself when we get back to London. Maybe all that was part of her fucking awful midlife crisis?* But I couldn't focus on her for long, the gnawing fear about what Antoni might do to me – or to anyone he knew I loved the most – was paralysing.

Half an hour later, I was in a bubble bath that Marie had run for me. I was sitting bolt upright, shivering, despite the hot water that surrounded me. My sister never travelled anywhere without her bag of cosmetics, lotions and potions, unlike me – who just packed the bare necessities. I wished so much that I could really wash all my troubles away. Just dissolve all my problems until they'd been sucked down the plughole. Create a time loop, go back and change the events of yesterday; stop

Antoni from seeing me downstairs. Change the fact that I'd heard him talk about the dead boy, Harvey.

An hour later, when I was a complete prune, I somehow made myself get out and get dressed.

I heard the front door open and close.

'Antoni?' Marie called from her bedroom next door. 'Is that you?'

'Who wants to know?' Antoni called back.

'Stay right where you are.' Marie walked out of her room and headed for the stairs. 'There's something I need to discuss with you...'

Chapter Thirty-Five

Marie and Antoni were in the smaller living room together for nearly an hour. I know because I was rigid with horrific expectation the whole time, not knowing what was going to happen, what he or she would say or do to each other. I was checking the time on my phone every few seconds. When they eventually reappeared, Antoni wasn't looking happy. I'd been standing at the top of the stairs, too scared to move, not wanting to overhear anything that I shouldn't again. When he reappeared, I made my way down the stairs.

'Your sister,' he said to me, spitting out each word, 'has convinced me that it would be best if you did the last interview for the book with me here in Wales this afternoon, and that we should all go back to London this evening. I'm not very fucking happy about this, but she's promised me that you'll get the last of the book typed up and emailed over to me and Sylvie by Monday morning.'

'Oh yes, I will,' I said. *Wow, could this really be true? Even after what I'd overheard? Were we actually going home? How could this be happening? I didn't need to steal the car keys and escape?* It felt too good to be true... 'Let's go and start the interview now, Antoni. And I absolutely promise that I'll finish typing it up over the weekend. The finished manuscript will be in Sylvie's inbox by Monday morning. You have my word.'

It felt like his eyes were boring into my soul. I had no idea what he was thinking. Then he nodded and turned towards our interview room.

'Thank you,' I mouthed at Marie. She grinned back and gave me the thumbs up. I kept wondering what she'd said to him to make him change his mind. It must have been huge – did she know about what he'd done to Harvey too? Had she threatened him with that? Antoni didn't seem the type to be intimidated by anyone so I doubted it, but I didn't know, couldn't be sure...

By half past four, Antoni had finished his story. We were done, and neither of us had addressed the awful situation that had happened the day before. But things had changed between us, the tension was almost too much to bear. However, an hour later, we were all packed up and back in Marie's car. Stitches and Joe Bull had called for a taxi, they were going somewhere different, and I wish I knew where, as I now knew how vile they were. Mine and Danny's safety had to come first, and I planned to ask Sylvie about them when I could. I kept thinking that at any moment, Antoni would call our departure off. Find some reason to make us stay...

Sylvie's free now, I kept thinking as I plugged my seat belt in. *And maybe I'll get paid what I'm owed. I'm going to see Danny. And so far Antoni is leaving me alone. Could there be a chance that he'll just trust me not to say anything to anyone about what he did to Harvey? He must know how fucking terrified I am...*

The traffic on the way home was awful. It was like everyone in Wales had decided to get on the roads. Then as we were stuck in yet another traffic jam, Antoni decided that he was hungry and ordered Marie to stop at the next services. While he and Marie selected their motorway snacks, Sylvie and I went outside to get some space. I'd tried to get Marie to come with us, wanted to talk to her about Antoni and how dangerous he was, warn her not to get any more involved with him. But she'd brushed me off.

'I'm starving, Poll,' she'd said, waving her hand in a vague way. 'I'm staying here. I'll see you guys in a bit.'

I strongly suspected that Antoni's eyes were staring at my back as we walked away. I decided to phone Dad. It was after 8pm by that stage.

'How's Danny?' I said as soon as my father answered the phone.

'Oh, very well,' Dad said in his quiet tones. 'He was awarded a certificate today in school. He's had a bath and has just fallen asleep on the sofa, Polly. I'll get him up to his room in a minute. Unless you're going to be back very soon, do you think it might be an idea if you come and collect him tomorrow morning?'

Tears immediately filled my eyes. *My baby had got a certificate and I hadn't been there to see it.*

'I think I'll come tonight, if that's okay, Dad,' I said. 'Long story, but I'd rather have Danny with me, even if that means I have to carry him to the car at one in the morning.'

'Well, all right,' my dad said. 'Safe travels. I'll see you later.'

I said goodbye and put my phone back into my pocket. *Eating again?* I thought as I saw Antoni wander back over to the fast food counter. I desperately wanted to get back on the road, but I also knew that Antoni was probably deliberately slowing the journey down as he wanted to punish me for what I'd heard. Letting me know that he was most definitely in charge. As long as I got back home to my son, it would be okay somehow. I could figure out my next steps once I was away from him. For now, I'd just have to grit my teeth and carry on being as patient as possible for the last few nightmarish hours...

Chapter Thirty Six

As I opened my eyes on Saturday morning and saw Danny's shock of golden hair lying next to me on the pillow, my heart had a little burst of joy, despite the ongoing horror I was feeling about Antoni. I was back with my beautiful child, after those five days from hell. But Christ, what a mess I'd – unwittingly – put us both in. I needed to protect my son. *Perhaps once I've sent the finished manuscript to Antoni we can go away on an impromptu holiday for a bit? Get a bit of space between us and that man for a while? Go somewhere that he doesn't have a clue about?* I was still paranoid to the hilt, my mind doing cartwheels as I tried to digest the implications about what I knew. But now that I was at home with Danny again, I had the chance to get back in control of my life...

No wonder he was still sleeping, I thought as I bent closer to inhale my son's freshly washed smell – hadn't Dad said he'd given him a bath the evening before? It had been nearly 2am by the time Marie had dropped me off at my house in Penge, and by the time I'd grabbed my keys and jumped in my Nissan Note before arriving at my dad's house in Bromley, it was getting on for 2.30am. I'd looked behind me all the way, driven much faster than I usually would, constantly worried that some sort of ramification was about to occur. But it hadn't. Which was very strange, really, as a man like Antoni surely didn't let things go quite so easily? I'd scooped Danny out of his warm bed, wrapped him in a blanket and laid him on the back seat of my car – strapping him in the best I could. He'd woken up once, and grinned when he'd seen me, and then fallen into a deep sleep again once I'd got him home and laid him in my bed.

If I could just get the damn book finished, Danny and I would be free to choose our next moves. And Sylvie could start rebuilding her life without that monster of a man – which was of course why I'd chosen to put myself through five days of hell in the first place. And I'd be able to work out some sort of plan, maybe move house? I thought. *We could move somewhere and not tell anyone our address? But all that would take time...*

When my son eventually awoke, and we went downstairs so I could fix him some breakfast, Danny was nattering away about the fabulous time he'd had with his grandad, and I tried my very hardest to concentrate on what he was saying, and not to let him catch on to the deep terror that was now permanently fixed in me...

'And he let me stay up later than you do,' he said. 'We watched *The A-Team* together. My favourite person in it is Hannibal.'

I made myself grin back, then went over to give my son yet another hug. Despite everything, I was so happy to be back with him again, something that – over the last few days – I'd thought may not be possible. I knew that I had to check up on Sylvie. I wanted to make sure Antoni was going to keep his promise to her, and leave her alone once he got the manuscript. If the worst happened, and Antoni went on terrorising her after he'd received it, then she'd have to get the police involved, I couldn't see any other way forward. Obviously the main – most horrific –

thing I had to get my head round was that I'd seen the aftermath to a murder. And the killer strongly suspected that I had too. So I was now permanently in danger, and the worst thing was not knowing what was going to happen. Maybe nothing – maybe Antoni knew that me being in permanent fear would be the worst punishment and deterrent that he could give me. On the other hand, he might do something. I didn't know. Those five days of being controlled by Antoni had been like a waking nightmare. I was now in no doubt about what a psychotic monster he was; a man with no conscience at all. A cold-blooded killer. If I even talked to the police, I had a feeling he would somehow find out. And then my life would be over. I had to keep my mouth shut and work out a plan for the near future. The other issues – including Marie working as a prostitute – would have to wait. I'd work out what to do about all those later. I'd texted her to make sure she'd got home okay, but had had no reply. I had to presume that all was well, as I was sure Henry would have contacted me if it wasn't.

Danny and I had the best day that we could together. We played his favourite games, watched his best DVDs. All the time, I was squashing down the fear inside me, constantly hypervigilant, jumping at every sound, twitching the curtains back and forth whenever a car stopped outside the house.

By 6pm my son was yawning – no doubt tired out from the day before. When I asked him if he'd like to sleep in my bed again as a special treat he jumped at the chance, and by 7pm he was snoozing soundly, his little head on my pillow. I went round the house, checking all the locks on the windows and doors for the umpteenth time.

Now, I thought, *I have a chance to finish Antoni's book. And I really need to do this, for all our sakes.* I'd phoned Marie a few times, wanting to talk to her about Antoni, make sure she knew how dangerous he was, and see if she knew anything about the murder. But she didn't pick up, so I'd sent her more texts. Her behaviour in Wales had hurt me, but she was still my sister and I needed to make sure she was safe. I was hoping she'd get back to me soon. I fished my Dictaphone and laptop out of my still unpacked travel bag, turned them both on, and set to work. It was the last thing I wanted to do, my head was all over the place, but it was the next step towards safety and freedom...

I was a fair way through the material when the doorbell rang. I nearly had a heart attack. *Fuck! Antoni?*

I was shaking as I pulled the living-room curtain back to take a peek at who was outside. I inhaled sharply. It wasn't Antoni, it was two people who were even more unexpected. Danny's father, Jakub, and what appeared to be – judging from the fact that she was clutching his hand – his new girlfriend.

Chapter Thirty-Seven

'Jakub?' I said, opening the front door. 'What are you doing here?'

Christ, I thought. *He looks awful.* I took in his pale skin, his sunken cheeks, his missing teeth. *What the hell has happened to him?* It had been over two years since we'd last seen each other, and the last time I'd clapped eyes on the man he'd certainly looked a lot healthier than this. His addiction to alcohol must really be taking its toll...

'We've come for the money,' the woman standing next to him said. 'How much can you lend us?'

I let my gaze wash over her. *Looks like a bitch.* She had peroxide-dyed hair with massive roots, her skin was bad – covered in spots and what seemed to be a rash – and she had tiny eyes that were staring at me with strong dislike, her mouth now twisted into a scowl.

'Absolutely nothing,' I said. The past few days had certainly reignited my old feistiness and there was no way I was going to let this woman or Jakub demand anything from me. And there was no way I was inviting the pair of them in to discuss it. The woman seemed hostile, and I didn't need any more of that kind of shit in my life. 'I'm sorry to tell you that I don't have any money at the moment. So you both need to go. And next time, phone me before you want to come over. Danny's asleep and I don't want anything to wake him up.'

'We need the money now,' the woman said. *Jesus. What did I need to do to get through to her?*

'Christine,' Jakub said, turning to her. 'Let me handle this.' He turned back to me. 'I'm so sorry to call on you like this, Polly,' he said. His eyes looked like dark, desperate holes. 'But we are in a dire financial situation at the moment and have exhausted all other possibilities. I know I haven't been great at paying anything towards Danny's upkeep recently...'

I snorted. *That was an understatement. Jesus, they had gall coming round here like this...*

'So I'm not asking for the money outright. More as a loan that I'll pay back as soon as I can.'

There was something not right about the pair of them, but I couldn't put my finger on exactly what it was. Something about their eyes... Then a memory came to me.

'Oh, Jakub,' I said. 'By the way, do you know two people called Sylvie and Antoni?' *Maybe I was playing with fire, asking this, but I had to know...*

I could tell immediately from his shocked expression that he knew exactly who I was talking about.

'No,' he said after a pause. 'I don't think so.'

'The money,' the woman said.

'Listen,' I said to her, leaning forwards. 'I don't know who you are, and right now I don't care. But how dare you just turn up on my doorstep on Saturday evening, demanding money that by rights should actually be put towards Jakub's child maintenance? I've had the worst week ever, and right now I just want to be by myself. You both need to leave now.'

'I'm so sorry, Polly,' Jakub said. 'We didn't mean to upset

you.' He took hold of the woman's hand and tried to pull her away. But she was clearly not having any of this. She yanked him back.

'We need it by Monday morning,' she said. 'And if you haven't transferred it to Jakub by then, then you'll regret not taking my words seriously. I promise you that.'

'Oh fuck off, will you?' I said, and slammed the door in their faces.

Jesus Christ, I thought, walking back over to my laptop. *I don't need this shit right now.*

I felt too rattled by my unwelcome visitors and the angry outburst that they had initiated in me to carry on with my work, but I knew I had to, if I was going to keep to the agreed schedule. And it was imperative that I did. I'd come this far for Sylvie, so I was determined to keep going. But it wasn't just about her now, it was about extricating myself from this psycho too. As soon as Antoni had the finished manuscript, I planned to contact Sylvie and make sure that he was keeping to his end of the bargain. And then I planned to somehow get away with Danny, and to try and think clearly about what to do next, whether to get the police involved, who to tell – if anyone – about Antoni and Harvey.

So I made myself a strong coffee – it was going to be a long night – and forced myself to sit back down at my laptop and turn on the Dictaphone again. One way or another, this fucking book was getting finished...

Chapter Thirty-Eight

I pinged the email off to Sylvie – as I didn't have any contact details for Antoni – with the completed manuscript attached to it at 4.20am on Monday morning. Then I texted her:

It's all done, Sylvie, and waiting for you in your inbox. Please let me know that Antoni is now sticking to his promise to leave you alone.

There were only three and a half hours until I needed to wake Danny up and get him ready for school, and I was insanely tired. But I didn't care, I was also elated. I'd done the impossible, written a whole book in a week. Made Antoni look like the hardest, baddest gangster that ever lived. His ego could feed off it for the rest of his life for all I cared, although I doubted that any publisher would take it on. He'd have to self-publish probably, and good luck with that. Although I knew how to go about doing that I certainly wasn't going to help him get his book live on Amazon, he could fumble through that process by himself. My job was done and posted to him. The manuscript was finished, and the resulting message in my 'Sent' folder proved this. And I knew that once I'd dropped Danny at school,

I could come home and sleep until about 2.45pm that day. The exhaustion was also dulling down the fear I had about the murder. Nothing had happened so far, so maybe it wasn't going to...

I took Danny to St Mary's School, gave him an extra-long hug, walked the short distance home, and flopped back into bed, ignoring yet another message from my sister. I had a deep, uninterrupted sleep until about half one, at which point the doorbell started ringing. Making my way down the stairs – with that strange unreal feeling flooding my brain that you get when you're suddenly woken up from daytime sleeping – I opened the front door, half expecting it to be Jakub and his new squeeze standing there again. But it was two police officers. And I could see their marked car on the road behind them. I blinked. My mind started reeling.

'Sorry to disturb you,' one of them said. 'It's nothing to worry about, but there's been an incident on the A213. The driver of a red Skoda Fabia has caused a bit of a pile-up – several people have injuries but luckily there are no fatalities. After looking at CCTV evidence, we have reason to believe he was speeding down your road shortly before he crashed. We're trying to find witnesses to this. Did you hear or see anything?'

'Um,' I said, trying to take all of this information in. My foggy mind was trying to think whether I knew anyone who drove a red Skoda Fabia. I couldn't think of anyone who did. 'No, sorry. I was working until late last night, so I've been sleeping for most of the day. I didn't hear anything, I'm afraid.'

'No worries at all,' the other officer said. 'You don't happen to have a CCTV camera fitted anywhere do you? We're looking for sightings of the car so that we can piece together the events that led up to the crash.'

I shook my head.

'No, I don't,' I said. *Although I should probably get one now...*

'No problem, sorry to have disturbed you,' the officer said, and they turned and walked back to their car.

Random, I thought, closing the door. I realised that I was shaking. I was living on my nerves. Expecting the worst. And it was hardly surprising.

I decided that a strong coffee was in order, and while the kettle was boiling I picked up my phone and stared at it. No text from Sylvie acknowledging the receipt of the manuscript. I sent her a text, asking if she'd seen the email. I needed closure on the whole thing as soon as possible, I didn't want there to be any reason for Antoni to say that I hadn't stuck to my end of the bargain.

A few minutes later, as I was placing the steaming mug – the biggest I could find – on the kitchen table, my phone pinged. It was a message from Sylvie.

Yes, thank you so much, Polly, we have received the book and Antoni is reading through it right now.

Thank fuck for that, I thought. I paused for a moment, then sent her another text:

I'm really pleased. Is he going to leave you alone now as promised? Sorry to ask, but if you could pay the money into my account by the end of today, that would be fantastic.

And then me and Danny can go away for a bit...

You're nearly there, Polly, I thought, putting the phone down again. *Keep going, make sure Sylvie is a free woman again. Make sure that Antoni is out of her and your life once and for all. You're nearly in a position to take charge of your life again, get yourself and Danny to a place of safety...*

Shit, I thought, putting my mug down and then bowing my head until it was cradled in my hands. *Why had life become so hard?* I looked up. *No, Polly*, I thought, shaking the thought away. *You're stronger now, you can deal with this. You're nearly there. Just think... what do you need to do now?*

I sat up a bit and took a sip of my coffee.

Dad, I decided. I needed to talk to him; warn him about the danger he could potentially be in. Antoni had made it quite clear that he knew about my father and Danny, and it was my number one priority to keep them safe. It would be a difficult conversation to have, but it was necessary. Better that Dad was shocked, rather than hurt further down the line.

I grabbed my phone and rang his landline.

'Hello?' His papery tones answered after six rings.

'Dad,' I said. 'Would it be okay if me and Danny come and see you after I get him from school today? There's something important that I need to discuss with you.'

'Yes of course,' he said immediately. 'Are you okay, Polly? Is everything all right?'

'Yes, sort of,' I said. 'Don't worry, Dad, I'll be fine. I could just do with bending your ear for an hour or so if that's okay with you. See you just after half three.'

We said our goodbyes, and I placed my phone back on the table. Good. I stared at the time on my phone – 2.17pm – and willed the afternoon to pass faster...

Chapter Thirty-Nine

Danny was very excited to be going back to Grandad's so soon. I'd brought a snack and a drink with me for him, as always, and he devoured these during the short car journey to Bromley.

Once we'd pulled up next to Dad's house, and I was waiting for my son to get out of the car, my phone pinged. I pulled it out of my pocket and looked at it. It was a message from Jakub:

I'm so sorry to bother you again, Polly, it said. *But Christine has asked me to remind you that she gave Monday morning as a deadline for you to transfer the money to me, and that it is now Monday afternoon.*

My brow furrowed as I stared at his words. Something wasn't right here, Jakub would never normally behave like this. Would never be so pushy and insistent. I'd known the man for years – although I was now doubting whether I'd really properly known anyone in my life. He'd never be so relentless and demanding normally. But he did have a weak side to him, and maybe this Christine person had got him wrapped round her little finger somehow. I was quite sure that it was Christine who wanted the money so badly, not Jakub, which was just one of the reasons that I had no intention of transferring it to him. I was also worried about Marie as she still hadn't got back to me, in fact neither had Sylvie. God, I hoped that she'd transfer me the payment that she'd promised. I felt awful that she was having to pay for Antoni's dirty work, but collecting my fee would be the only way that I could take my son away for a few days...

'Come on, Mummy,' Danny said, grabbing my hand and dragging me up the path towards Dad's front door. 'You're staying here with me this time, aren't you?'

'Yes, darling, I most certainly am,' I said, leaning down to kiss the top of his head.

Minutes later, Dad and I were sitting in his living room – cups of tea in our hands – and Danny had gone out into the garden 'to do more exploring in the jungle'.

'So,' Dad said. 'What's up, Polly?'

It was like a soothing balm, sitting there with Dad in the living room that had barely changed since I was a child. Just hearing his kind voice had triggered off some sort of release deep within me. I collected my thoughts, and then began to explain the situation to him as best I could. I felt a bit ashamed about the mess I'd got into, felt awful that it now involved him. But glad that I was able to warn him about the potential danger.

'You probably won't believe half of what I've got to tell you,' I began, then stopped. Dad got up and came to sit next to me.

'Try me,' he said, placing a hand on my back.

So my words began tumbling out, and I told him about everything. How Sylvie was an amazing lady who'd survived so much abuse and gone on to thrive and be a successful businesswoman, but how she'd got back in touch with her violent ex-partner when he'd got out of jail, after he convinced her that he'd changed for the better. How this man had soon gone back to his criminal ways, taking and selling drugs, being aggressive and violent. How she'd sent their son to live with some family friends to get him out of the horrible atmosphere. Then, how Antoni had found out that I was writing a book about Sylvie's life story, and how he'd totally hijacked the project, wanting it to be about him instead, was convinced that because I'd written a bestseller before I'd be able to make him an infamous megastar overnight just by writing about him. How he saw pound signs rolling off the book once it was published, and how he wanted it to make him look like a mad and bad gangster that everyone would respect and fear. How he was narcissistic and egotistical and cared about no one but himself.

'He wanted me to go away with them to Wales last week,' I said. 'You know, that's why you had Danny to stay with you here, Dad. But terrible things happened once we were all there, two of Antoni's gang friends turned up too, and all they did was smoke crack and party. Antoni kept going away from the house "on business", as he said, which delayed me finishing the book as he was never there for me to interview. So he then said I had to stay in Wales with him indefinitely. And when I said no, I needed to get back to my son, he recited your address – word for word – to show me that he knew exactly where you and Danny were. It was a threat, to make me do what he wanted. But luckily Marie managed to convince him – somehow – that we all needed to get back on Friday evening, and he eventually agreed if I promised that I would deliver the completed manuscript to him by this morning. Which I managed to do. He said that he'd leave Sylvie alone once I'd sent him the completed project, but she hasn't replied to my most recent message and I'm getting worried. Basically, I came here to warn you about Antoni, Dad. That you might be in danger too, now that he knows your address. Maybe you can come away with me and Danny, if I get paid what I'm owed? We can all hide out somewhere for a while, and hope that this mess blows over, and that Antoni's focus gets directed elsewhere...'

Dad stared at me for a long moment. Then he breathed out.

'Polly,' he said. 'You should have gone to the police. You should have told me what was happening.'

'No,' I said, shaking my head. 'No, Dad. You don't understand. I can't get the police involved. Antoni is such a dangerous individual, and he's already used my son to threaten me. I need to think about the best thing to do before we make any decisions like that. I need to keep you, Danny and Marie safe first and foremost. Trust me on this.'

Dad's sharp eyes regarded me sadly.

'What a horrendous situation for you to be in, Polly,' he said. 'I'm so sorry you had to go through all that.'

I hadn't told Dad about the fact that Marie had been selling her body for money. I couldn't put that amount of stress on him. I desperately wanted to tell him that I was pretty sure I knew who murdered Harvey. But it wasn't right to do that.

But I did tell him all about Jakub and Christine, and how they'd turned up on my doorstep demanding money. I showed him the text that Jakub had sent me as a reminder that day.

Dad's eyebrows lowered as he reached for his glasses, and then stared at my phone screen.

'Stupid man,' he said, shaking his head. 'Don't pay him, Polly. What's he playing at?'

I knew that Dad didn't approve of Jakub's rather lax parenting skills at the best of times, and he'd never had much time for 'waifs and strays', as he called them, who seemed to feel entitled to parasitically live off other people.

We chatted on for a bit, and I began to feel the suffocating weight lift off me – just a fraction. Dad was putting things into perspective; he pointed out that my nightmare with Antoni was now over, and that Sylvie was probably fine and too busy with her bistro to contact me, and that I could put the whole horrible thing behind me. He said Jakub was too spineless to continue to contact me about the money for much longer, and that I should just keep being strong about that.

'Thanks, Dad,' I said, leaning over to give him another hug. 'I'm feeling a bit better for talking to you. I think I just needed to get all the stress out, and for someone to listen.'

'Not at all,' he said. 'Any time, Polly. And remember, the worst is past now. I'm sure you'll hear back from Sylvie this evening. Just be more careful about who you take on as writing clients in the future.'

I smiled.

'God, I definitely will,' I said, standing up. 'I've learnt my lesson there. Although I feel proud to have worked with Sylvie, Dad, and to have been able to help her. Who knows, in the future we may even be able to get her story down on paper. It will inspire so many people. But for now I think I'll just stick to the Ghostwriting Team, as they vet all their customers before passing them on to us writers.'

'Good idea.' Dad struggled to his feet. 'Right, let's go and find that son of yours.'

We walked through to the kitchen, and then out into the large, overgrown garden. I grinned. My son was probably nestled in one of his many 'hideouts', which were usually within old bushes or under broken fence panels.

'Danny,' I called. 'It's time to go home. Come and say goodbye to Grandad.'

No answer. I waited for a while, expecting my grinning son to pop his head up somewhere any minute. But everything in the garden remained still and quiet.

'Danny?' I called again, louder this time. 'Come on, out you come.'

Still no answer. There was no movement at all among the leaves. I waited, wondering...

A jolt of panic whooshed through me. Was he hurt?

'Danny?' My voice was higher now. 'Don't play games please, sweetheart, you're making Mummy worried...'

Still no answer. I set off through the undergrowth, staring wildly under things, on top of bushes, looking behind the shed, the broken fence, up the trees. I even looked under plants that were far too small for him to be under. I looked over the fences, in case – for some bizarre reason – he'd decided to climb over one of those. But there was no sign of Danny anywhere. And the outdoor space was too quiet. Too still.

'Danny,' Dad was calling. 'It's time to come out now.'

I walked round the garden six times, checking absolutely everywhere over and over again, an uncontrolled sense of panic now coming into full force in my brain. Where was my son?

'Danny?' I shouted. 'Come on, darling, this isn't funny anymore. You have to come out now.'

'He's not here, Dad,' I said, turning towards my father. I was finding it hard to breathe. 'He's not here. He'd have come out now if he was. And anyway, I'd have found him. But he's not here.'

'Check the back gate,' Dad said, and I ran towards it. The gate was about waist high, and slightly ajar. Why would it be like that? It was always kept shut. It was the one barrier between that bit of the garden, and then the driveway, pavement and road. Danny had never shown much interest in it before, and he'd always been under strict instructions never to open it and go out. He'd always been so good at not doing that. Up till now...

I opened the gate, ran down the driveway, and onto the pavement. I stared this way and that.

'Danny?' I shouted, as loudly as I could. 'Danny? Where are you?'

Nothing, no little boy appeared. Some people in cars turned their heads and stared at me as they drove past.

'He's gone, Dad!' I screamed. 'Danny's gone. He's not here.'

'Phone the police,' Dad said, a look of horror on his face. And with a shaking hand I somehow retrieved my phone from my pocket. I was about to punch in the three nines, when a text popped up on my screen. It was from an unknown number:

Do not call the police. Danny is safe. You will soon receive instructions on what to do next.

Chapter Forty

My head was swimming. I was sitting on the pavement, leaning against Dad's front wall. I couldn't breathe.

'Polly,' Dad was saying. 'Polly, come back into the house.'

But I couldn't move. I couldn't see properly. Someone had taken my son. My precious boy. My worst fear – my absolute worst nightmare – was taking place. And I was powerless to do anything. I leant to one side and threw up.

'Polly,' Dad said loudly. 'Come on, get up. Come back into the house and we can work out what to do next.'

I wiped my mouth, an automatic movement. When I look back, I don't know how I did this, but somehow I ended up back in Dad's living room. Time was very fluid, unreal at that point. This wasn't my life, it was someone else's. There was no way that my son could be missing, was there? I was going to wake up soon...

'Polly,' Dad was saying. 'I know this is horrific, but you have to try and focus so that we can go about getting Danny back. If we can't go to the police then we'll have to find a way ourselves.' He'd always been calm in a crisis. But when I looked up at him, I saw how much pain he was really in.

'Yes,' I repeated. 'Get Danny back.'

'Can you think of anyone who'd take him?' Dad said. 'Think carefully.'

'Antoni,' I said, pain – like I'd never felt before – ripping through me. I was in no doubt that he'd taken my son. 'Antoni is very dangerous.'

'Or maybe Jakub?' Dad said, standing up and shuffling towards his laptop. 'He and his new girlfriend were the ones threatening you about money, weren't they? Let's eliminate problems and if that doesn't work we will have to phone the police, despite what that text said. I'll transfer you the five hundred, and you can pay it to Jakub right now.'

I sat there dumbly while Dad transferred the money to me. And then – with robotic movements – I brought up online banking and paid the money into Jakub's account.

'Call him now, Polly,' Dad said. 'Let the man know that he now has his money. If it was him and that woman who took Danny as a threat, then they have no reason to keep hold of him any longer.'

I found Jakub's number and rang it.

'Hello?' he answered after one ring. 'Polly?'

'Have you taken Danny?' I said, my voice becoming a wail. 'Have you got Danny with you, Jakub? Please tell me the truth. I'm sick with worry.'

'What?' he said, sounding confused. 'No, of course not.'

'Well,' I carried on. 'I've just transferred you the money you wanted. So if you do have Danny, please can you drop him back at my dad's house now. Please, please, Jakub?'

'Polly,' he said, sounding worried now. 'I don't have Danny. He's with you.'

'No he's not,' I said between sobs.

'Thank you for the money,' Jakub said. 'And I'm so sorry to have to ask you for it, Polly. Is Danny okay? What's going on?'

I cut him off and ended the call.

'He says he doesn't have him,' I said, my breaths shallow. 'I don't know if he's telling the truth, Dad. I don't know what to do.' Helplessness, like I'd never known before, had taken me over.

I just sat there. The phone fell from my fingers and onto the floor.

Then it bleeped into life.

I picked it up. It was Marie. I answered it.

'Danny's gone,' was the first thing I said to her. 'Oh, Marie, do you have any idea where he is?'

'Listen,' she said, speaking quietly. 'Where are you, Polly?'

'I'm at Dad's house,' I said.

'I know that Antoni's taken Danny,' she said.

I felt dizzy. I was right. That monster had my son.

'That fucking psycho has Danny?' I said.

'Yes,' Marie said. 'He's really pissed at you, Polly. He's had your house watched since we all got back from Wales, he said he didn't trust you. That you were the weak link among us. I don't really understand what he's talking about, but he's furious. He knows that police came to your house today and he thinks it must have been because you have told them something about him. He says there's no way he's going back to jail. That's why he's taken Danny. He wants you to know that you have to stop talking to the police about him.'

'What?' I said, my thoughts spinning. 'The police came by to see me because of a speeding incident. Someone came down my road too fast and crashed into other people on the A213. They were just looking for witnesses.'

There was a pause.

'I'll try and get a message to Sylvie about that,' Marie said. 'All I know is that you're in serious danger, Polly. Antoni wants to frighten you to the point where you never say anything about him to the authorities ever again. He said that he has lots of dead bodies around him that no one knows about, and that he's not afraid to add another one to the pile.'

'But I haven't,' I whispered. 'I promise I haven't. You have to believe me, Marie.'

'You're in danger, Polly,' Marie said. 'Serious danger. Antoni's planning on coming after you next; he wants to teach you to leave his business alone. He said to Sylvie that snitches get stitches today, and he was talking about you.'

Chapter Forty-One

'What?' I said. I felt like I was going to faint.

'Listen to what I'm going to say to you now very carefully,' Marie said, her voice very low. 'Go back to your house, and pack up what you need for a week or two. I know I haven't been a very good sister lately, but I'm going to make up for that now by protecting you the best that I can, Polly. You need to get away from your house, otherwise you're just a sitting duck. Don't tell Dad what I'm saying, just do it. Okay?'

'But Danny...' I began.

'Once you're safe we'll figure out a way to get Danny back safe and sound,' Marie said. 'I'm sure Sylvie will help us. But don't phone her or Antoni today, he needs time to calm down before we contact him. Do what I said first, all right? We need to get you out of harm's way, and then we can get Danny home.'

She said goodbye and rang off.

What the actual fuck? Antoni had taken my son and now he was after me?

I stood up.

'Polly?' Dad said. 'What are you doing? Who was that? You've gone even paler than you were before.'

'I'm really sorry, Dad, but I have to go,' I said. 'That was Marie. I can't tell you any more at the moment, but I'll fill you in as soon as I can.'

Dad's face was full of anguish.

'Keep me in touch with what's going on,' he said as I left.

I drove back to my house on autopilot. I hadn't unpacked most of the travel bag that I'd taken to Wales, so I just threw a few more bits of clothing into it, along with my phone charger. This was someone else's life, I was sure of it. I'd accidentally slipped through a hole in the universe and ended up where I shouldn't be. Very soon, things would be put right and go back to normal. Maybe I was having a fucking awful nightmare. I stopped what I was doing and pinched myself. No, I was pretty sure that I wasn't dreaming. If I was, I wanted to wake up right now... I made myself finish the packing and went to wait downstairs.

Very soon, I heard Marie pull up outside. I opened the front door.

'Get in,' she said. 'Quick, Polly. We don't have much time.' She looked about as though she was expecting someone to be watching us.

I did as she said. My mind was going by that stage, I knew it was. I'd begun the descent into madness, and at the moment there was no way out of it... Somehow, I clambered into the passenger seat next to her and went through the motions of fastening my seat belt.

We drove in silence for what must have been over an hour. Me a shaking, dribbling mess and Marie grim-faced and for once – silent. Every now and again I half lost consciousness and entered a hallucinatory kind of dream state. I could hear Danny calling my name, but I couldn't see him anywhere. When I came to again, silent tears were pouring down my cheeks. Shit, the fact that I'd dreamt something and woken up meant that this wasn't just a horrific nightmare that I was living through. It was actually happening.

It was pitch black outside. I had no idea where we were as I couldn't concentrate on the signs that we whizzed past. I didn't care where we were. I didn't care about anything except getting my son back. Another hour passed, and I saw signs for Swindon, then Chippenham, then Bristol, but I felt like we were driving into hell.

Finally, the car began to slow down.

'We're here,' Marie said. She turned off the satnav on her phone. I stared through the window and saw a nondescript terraced cottage illuminated by the orange light of a lamp post. 'In Glastonbury Town in Somerset. I've rented this place for you, with some of the earnings I've made over the last month. It's cheap and cheerful but it will do you for now. Only you and I know that you'll be staying here, so you'll be completely safe. It's an Airbnb. You get the key out of the safety box outside, I'll just check what the code is...'

She fished out her phone and scrolled through a couple of pages.

'Nine, one, four, three,' she said. 'Have you got that, Polly? Nine, one, four, three. I'm going to have to go now, but I'll come back first thing tomorrow morning. And don't worry about Danny, I'm sure Antoni will keep him safe. He's not angry with your son, he's pissed at you. I'm not sure why, I don't understand it but I'll come and talk to you about it tomorrow, okay?'

I grabbed my bag, got out of the car and punched the code into the box that was screwed into the wall at the side of the door. It flipped open, and I took out the key.

'I'll see you in the morning,' Marie said, revving the engine. 'Look after yourself, Polly.'

'Wait,' I said, turning. 'Marie, what's really going on here? Do you know something else – more than I do? I mean, you've been spending so much time with Antoni and his friends. Do you know about the boy Harvey Grant who was murdered in London?'

My sister stared at me for a moment, unblinking, her expression unreadable.

'Look, I can't talk now, I have to go,' she said. 'But we'll carry on with this conversation tomorrow, okay?'

And with that, she turned her head away and drove off.

Chapter Forty-Two

The next day, after a night of little sleep, I was up and ready to get my son back. No matter what it took. I just needed to work out what the fuck was really going on...

So, I thought. *If Antoni has Danny, and he was the one who texted me yesterday telling me not to go to the police, then I can reach him directly on that number. I know that Marie said not to contact him or Sylvie, but today is a new day. And I need to do something. But I need to be careful, I don't want to make him more angry than he already is. I need to negotiate with him, try and work out a place for him to safely release Danny back to me...*

I picked up the phone and called the number that was on yesterday's text. It just rang and rang. No voicemail, no answer. I let it ring over fifty times, willing Antoni to pick up.

Okay, I thought, eventually pressing the red button. *He clearly doesn't want to talk to me. I'll send him a message instead.*

I thought for a minute, then typed:

Antoni, please, please just let me know that Danny is safe and well. I promise you that I won't tell anyone anything that I know about your life.

I pressed send, and the text flew away into the ether. I wasn't demanding much to start with, just a brief message to let me know how my son was. I hadn't addressed overhearing anything about Harvey, just a general promise of complete confidentiality.

A wave of dizziness overtook me. What had happened was unthinkable. Beyond criminally horrendous. Yet the fucking man had me in a double bind; he was using the fact that he had my son – with the implied threat being that he'd do awful things to him – if I went to the police. So what was I supposed to do? Think, Polly, think...

I picked up my phone again. I'd call Sylvie and beg her – implore her – to take Danny away from Antoni and bring him back to me safely. She was a mother for Christ's sake, she must be able to imagine the utter devastation and heartache that I was feeling right now...

I pulled up her number and tapped on it. But all I could hear was the monotonous ringing tone going on and on. *Maybe Antoni had taken her phone off her?* I thought. Or maybe she was in on this evil plan too? I just didn't know anymore, everything in my world had been shattered and I could trust no one...

A loud knocking on the front door made me jump.

'Polly?' Marie's voice called. 'It's me. Can you come and let me in?'

I went and opened the door. Marie took one look at me and blinked.

'Fuck me,' she said. 'You look awful. What the hell did you do to yourself?'

'Hardly slept,' I said, standing aside so that she could come in. 'Not surprising really, is it?'

'Well,' my sister said, barging past me and leaving a freshly washed smell floating behind her, 'this whole thing must be cutting you up. It's about the worst thing that can happen to a mother. I just don't understand why Antoni has done this.'

I'd cried so much over the last twenty-four hours that my tear ducts felt all dried up. If they were in better working order, I would have burst into hysterics again at that point.

'I wanted to come and check on you,' Marie said, filling up the kettle. 'Before I go and meet Sylvie. She's as distraught as you and I are, Poll...' I doubted that very much, but I said nothing. 'She said that Antoni's never done anything as awful as this – to her knowledge – before,' Marie went on. *But he's just axed a seventeen-year-old to death,* I thought. *If he's done that, then he's capable of anything...* 'She just can't understand it. I told her that the police only came to call on you to ask about a speeding driver, and she said she'd tell Antoni. We're meeting in Downham, far away from Beckenham and Crystal Palace as possible, so that hopefully Antoni or his gang mates won't spot us. I can't stay here long as it will take me a couple of hours to drive over there.'

'You actually spoke to Sylvie?' I said. *This was a good sign, surely? But if she spoke to Marie then why wasn't she picking up the phone to me? I was more in need of reassurance about my son than my sister...*

'Only briefly,' Marie said. 'We couldn't talk for long. Danny's not at their house by the way so there's no point in anyone sending the police over to look.'

'Well where is he then?' I said, my voice hoarse. 'My poor Danny. God, Marie. I'm so fucking terrified.'

'I know you are, bless you,' my sister said. She was in practical mode with her back to me, making us both a hot drink.

'I'll do my very best to find out as much as I can from Sylvie, and I'll let you know as soon as she tells me anything, okay?'

'And please tell her to reassure Antoni that although I don't know much about his life, I won't breathe a word about anything I do know to anyone, especially to the police. Everything is safe with me, I'll keep it all confidential. It's really important that you get that message to him, okay?' I didn't want to confess to knowing about Harvey to anyone, because admitting it outright might cause Antoni to silence me once and for all.

'Thank you,' I said, wiping my eyes as she placed a coffee in front of me. 'And thanks for keeping me safe, Marie. I honestly don't know what I would have done without you.'

Marie gave a small smile.

'That's what sisters do, isn't it?' she said. 'Look out for each other. And I'm sorry about last week, Polly. I know it must have been a real shock for you to find out that I was doing escort work. I had actually planned not to tell you, but I was stupid and got too drunk when we were in Wales. Letting off steam, I think. Not exactly behaving like a responsible older sister, am I?'

'Don't worry about it,' I replied. 'Like you just said, sisters always look out for each other. I'll always be there for you, Marie.'

The look that crossed her face was strange.

'Thank you, Poll,' she said. 'Now drink up. That's a very strong coffee and it will help you wake up properly. You need to be in top shape for when we get Danny back, don't you?'

'Yep.' I nodded. My sister was right, I needed to get myself as strong as possible for my son. I took a big sip of coffee, then watched as Marie chugged hers down quickly.

'Now I must go, Polly,' my sister said. 'I don't want to be late to meet Sylvie as I don't know how much time we'll have together. Antoni – obviously – doesn't know that she's coming to meet me.'

'God, of course,' I said, standing up to see her out. 'Please let me know as soon as you hear anything, Marie. Please. I'm finding all this too hard to bear. It's too horrific...'

'Of course I will.' Marie squeezed my arm before turning towards the doorway. 'Stay strong, Poll.'

Seconds later, she was back in her car and driving away.

Oh God, I thought. *How the fuck am I going to get through the day waiting for news about Danny? Surely there must be something that I can do?*

Chapter Forty-Three

I finished my coffee, then went and sat on the small, upright sofa. I stared into space. This was possibly the worst day of my life. I felt helpless, at the mercy of others – mostly Antoni. I was Danny's mother, I was supposed to protect him, make sure no harm ever came to him. What a shit job I'd made of that. And yet I'd tried so hard to be a good mum to him. How could things turn out so horribly wrong?

Jesus, I thought. My head was going, a sense of wooziness was filling it. The room in front of me was taking on a watery quality, it seemed to be waving gently from one side to another.

I tried to stand up, thinking that some fresh air might sort me out. But I couldn't get my balance enough to get up on my feet. This was weird. It didn't feel right. There was something wrong with my body. But what was causing it? Probably the stress brought on by my son's abduction. *Christ I must be making myself unwell with all the worrying...*

I wanted to phone Brigitte, fill her in on all the awful things that were happening, hear her comforting warm tones. But I didn't even have the energy to pick up my phone...

I felt my eyelids closing, I was powerless to resist their pull. *Maybe I just need to sleep this off*, was the last thing I thought, before unconsciousness took me over...

Chapter Forty-Four

The relentless ringing of my phone cut through my numbed oblivion. I managed to open my eyes, and saw darkness outside the window. *Jesus, how long have I been asleep for? Was it night-time now? It must be past 6pm at least...* My head was throbbing and my vision still blurry. All the movements I made took more effort than usual, as though the air around me had become full of invisible treacle. I picked up my phone. It was Marie.

'Hello?' I said. Weird, my voice sounded strange.

'Polly,' she said. She sounded frantic. 'Antoni's found out where you are. He knows that you're at that address in Glastonbury and he's on his way to find you. The last thing Sylvie heard him say to his friend was that he was going to go and teach a snitch a lesson. You have to get out of there.'

'What?' My thoughts weren't processing. 'What do you mean?' My voice was coming out thick, like my tongue was swollen.

'Get out of the house,' Marie said. 'The cottage you're in is just in front of Glastonbury Tor, which is surrounded by undergrowth and trees. He'll never find you if you go up there.

Run, Polly. I don't know how much time you've got until Antoni gets to you.'

I put the phone down, but I wasn't feeling scared as my emotions, thoughts and physical self still felt completely numb. I tried to make sense of what Marie had told me, but her words were fading. I wanted to go back to sleep again, my eyelids were shutting...

No, I thought, forcing myself to sit up a bit more. I had to deal with this, for Danny's sake. When he was eventually found he would need a mother that was in one piece. *So Antoni was on his way, was he? Right, in that case I needed to stand up.*

I managed this – eventually – with much difficulty. I stood there by the sofa for a moment, swaying, trying to recall what else Marie had said. Get out of the house, she'd told me. Go where Antoni can't find you. Hadn't she said something about trees and bushes being behind the house? Right, then that's where I needed to be.

I reached down, picked up my phone, glancing at the messages and missed calls from Dad. Weird that I hadn't heard them come through. I'd have to reply to him later, when I was safe and also when I was feeling clearer headed than I was in my current state. I stuffed the phone into the pocket of my jeans, and headed for the front door and opened it. I pushed the key down into another pocket, and then set off – feeling sick and exhausted – into the night.

I had no idea where I was going, I'd never been to Glastonbury before and there was barely any street lighting to show me where to walk. The few lamp posts that there were shone their soft orangey glow down onto the uneven paving stones but I felt like I was in a dream world. No one else was around, as far as I could tell. God knows what time it was. Now, how was I supposed to get to these bushes and trees behind the house?

As I wandered along, unable to go very fast due to the malaise in my head and body, I saw an alleyway between two blocks of terraced housing. I had no sense of urgency, the numbing effect had taken all of that – and the fear and panic – away. I decided that I might as well go up the alley as it was as good a place as any to get away from the main streets. So that's what I did. And as I came to the end of it, what street lighting there was faded away and I found myself in pitch blackness.

I inched further along, arms out, hearing twigs start to snap under my feet. I had enough wits about me to realise that it would be a bad idea to turn the light of my phone on, because if Antoni was out there somewhere looking for me, it would be like a beacon for him. The last thing I wanted to do was to draw attention to myself.

I suddenly realised how cold the night air was. I hadn't even thought about bringing my coat with me, all I had on were my jumper and jeans. At that point, the clouds above cleared away from the moon, and for about twenty seconds the pale light illuminated a giant hill-like mound that rose up in front of me. Was this what Marie had been talking about? What had she called it – Glastonbury Tor? Okay, well at least I knew where I was heading now.

As the clouds regrouped and darkness took over once more, I kept walking ahead slowly, feeling branches and twigs sticking into my arms, body and legs from both sides now. These hurt, and I would no doubt be covered in deep scratches afterwards, but that was a small price to pay...

Then I heard a rustling sound near me. *Footsteps?* I stopped and held my breath. Twigs cracked as the rustling came closer. *He's found me*, I thought. Then a loud crack, an immense shooting pain at the back of my head. My eyes closed as I plummeted towards the ground.

Chapter Forty Five

I came to, still surrounded by blackness. My head felt like it had been split in half, the pain was indescribable. *Am I dying?* I thought. *Is this how I'm going to go?* An image of Danny flashed through what was left of my broken mind. *No, I was going to fight for my son till the bitter end. In whatever capacity that I could. But where was I?*

I could still move my hands despite them being tied. I felt around, and found that I was lying on some very thin carpet-like material. I was in a tight space. Bumping around. I was in the boot of a car.

Antoni's car? I thought, wincing as my head moved a fraction to the right. *I didn't think he had one? He's probably nicked Sylvie's one. He doesn't care about who he uses, or how often. Fucking evil man. I'll kick him in the face when he opens the boot.*

But as I tried to move my squashed legs, I realised that my ankles had been tied together. *Bastard. Never mind, I'll have to use both legs at the same time. More difficult, but I'll manage it. I'll just keep an image of Danny in my mind, and I'll be able to overcome anything.*

The numbing effects from whatever it was had worn off and electric fear laced by deep anger was throbbing through my body. I had no idea how long I'd been out cold for, or what time or day it was, or where we were going. But I was ready to fight now. I'd had enough. This fucker wasn't going to kill me as easily as he clearly thought he was. I had tunnel vision, I was going to be reunited with my son, whatever it took. Feisty Polly was back with full force, and then some. Woe betide that psychopath if he tried to do anything to me...

From the way I'd started to roll more from side to side, it felt like we were going off-road now, and over uneven ground. Wetness started slopping down over my forehead. *Was it sweat?* I wondered. *No, it was too cold for that. It was probably blood.* But I didn't care. The anger was overtaking the icy fear now. How dare he do this to me? I'd never done anything to him to deserve being treated like this. In fact, I'd spent hours writing that godawful book, praising his criminal exploits to high heaven. For no payment. And this is how he thanked me?

We were slowing down. I tensed the muscles in my legs, getting ready to bring them up in one swift movement and kick him in the face as hard as I could. I waited, holding my breath, listening to the car grind to a halt, the engine being turned off, a car door opening and then slamming, footsteps coming round to the boot...

There was a clunk, the boot lid was lifted and moonlight filtered through onto my face. I brought my feet up hard...

Then stopped.

It wasn't Antoni standing there.

Chapter Forty-Six

'Marie?' I said. 'What the fuck are you doing here?'

The shock made me freeze. *Surely I was imagining this? It couldn't be my sister standing in front of me, it just couldn't...*

'Oh little Pollyanna,' she said. 'Have I given you a surprise? Good, that's what I wanted. Now let's get you out of there.'

I didn't have time to boot her in the face. Seeing my sister standing there glaring at me had totally blindsided me. I couldn't move. Too many emotions were rushing through me: shock, betrayal, realisation...

She was too quick for me, she took advantage of my stunned state. As I watched her lean towards me – the night sky now clear of clouds – I saw that her eyes were dark; venomous. Murderous, even.

'What have I done to make you do this to me?' I said. *Why would my own sister hate me this much? It was Antoni who'd taken Danny. Wasn't it? Were they working together now?*

But she just gave me a sickly smile.

'Marie?' I said, feeling her name choke in my throat. 'Please don't do this. Let's talk about whatever is upsetting you. I'm sorry if I've done something. Please, let's calm down and we can sort whatever it is out. Like we've always done in the past.'

'Too late for that,' my sister said with a snarl in her voice. 'You still don't understand, do you? You little innocent.'

She yanked me into a sitting position, then threw me over the side of the boot. I put my tied hands out as best I could but whacked into the stony ground hard nevertheless. Pain flooded through me. My hands and face were now riddled with sharp gravel. I tried to sit up, but my sister kicked me back down.

'Why are you doing this, Marie?' I said, trying to turn my head so that I could look at her. *Had she gone mad? Was she on crack, like Antoni and his friends? Nothing would surprise me anymore.*

'Because you're ruining my life, Pollyanna.' She spat the words out.

'But how?' I said. 'What have I done?' I began racking my brains for signs, clues that I'd missed, that had led up to this moment. *I mean, yes, she'd hated me when we were children. But that was years ago. We were adults now.*

Marie walked round and stopped in front of me. I looked up and saw her towering above me.

'Hmm, let's see,' she said. 'When I was at Dad's house a couple of months ago, looking for my old clubbing photos as Sylvie had said she'd like to see them, guess what I found?'

'I don't know,' I said, hating this woman who I'd always loved.

'A copy of Dad's will,' she said. 'It was in the attic, in a box. Everything's a mess up there and I couldn't find any of my stuff. But I did find the will. And guess what it said, darling sister?'

'I have no idea,' I said. 'I've never seen it.' I was being honest, I hadn't. I hated the idea of Dad dying, it had been too awful losing Mum. I shied away from anything to do with funerals or death.

'It says that when Dad dies, the majority of the inheritance goes to you. I get the house, but you get everything else. All his and Mum's savings. Now, I'm sure you're far too innocent to know how much this amounts to, but let me tell you. It's just shy of four hundred thousand. And guess how much the house is worth? In the state it's in, not more than two fifty. He was going to favour you, even in death.'

'Favour me?' I said. 'What are you talking about, Marie? Dad loves us both equally.'

She laughed. It was a horrible sound.

'Really?' she said. 'Are you sure about that? He's always loved you more, Polly.'

'So was it you that took Danny from his garden, not Antoni?' I said. The fire and anger was building in me fast, replacing my initial shock. 'You're treating me like this because of money? And petty childhood squabbles? I can't believe it. You've got a fucking screw loose, Marie. You need help. And you've actually taken my son from me? You'd sink to those depths just to get a bit more cash?' *I'd be prepared to kill her first if it meant I'd get my son back...*

'Yes,' she said. 'I hadn't planned to. It was a spur-of-the-moment decision.'

'Are you mad?' My voice was rising now. 'Marie, that week in Wales with you all felt like an eternity in hell. It was fucking torture. But I still tried to contact you afterwards to make sure you were okay, and to warn you about Antoni. And you still took my son? Because you wanted a bigger share of the inheritance?'

'I wanted to teach you a lesson,' Marie said. 'Goody two-shoes Polly who everyone prefers. When I was driving back home from seeing a customer, and saw your car parked outside

Dad's house, I decided to see if Danny was in the garden. I know he spends most of his time out there in that "jungle" as he calls it. He's told me about all the fun he has out there on numerous occasions. He came running over when he saw me by the back gate. I told him that Bella was in the car and that she'd love it if he came to say hello. That she had a bag of sweeties, and that I was sure she'd share them with him. It was all so easy. I bundled him in, and told him that we were going on an adventure. And off we drove.'

'You fucking bitch!' I was screaming now. 'You had no right to take my son. Where is he? Where's Danny?' I tried to stand up but Marie kicked me back down again hard.

'He's safe,' my sister said. 'He's fine. But you don't need to worry about him anymore, Polly. When you're gone, I'll adopt him. He's always wanted Bella and Oliver to be his siblings after all. And then when Dad dies I'll inherit everything. I'll be able to pay off all our debts, and give Henry, the children and I a good life. Better than you could ever provide. And Dad doesn't like being alive anymore, does he? Anyone with an ounce of sense can see that; he's so shrivelled and depressed-looking now, and has been since Mum died. If it takes a helping hand from me to free him up from this life, then so be it. And that will mean I'll get my inheritance pretty soon. When Sylvie told me about Antoni, the whole plan came to me. How I could get you involved with him, and then frame the whole thing on him later on. Genius, if you ask me.'

'I want my son back now!' I said, my words coming out in one big screech. *So now Marie had plans to end our father's life too? What kind of fucking monster had my sister become? She'd planned the whole thing from the start – used Antoni and me so that she could frame him? Was she really this cold? This greedy?* I summoned every last bit of energy that I had and forced myself upright. Then, with my hands and feet still tied together, I threw myself at Marie, cannoning in to her. She fell backwards, slamming down hard onto the ground. I fell on top of her and tried to clumsily grab her arms with my tied hands. I wanted to hold her down, to shout in her face, make her realise how fucking stupid she was to be doing this. I wanted her to tell me exactly where Danny was so that I could go and get him. I still had my phone in my pocket, didn't I? If only I could get her to keep still then I could try and reach for it and phone the police. But my sister was too strong for me. And she had the advantage of having free hands and feet. It didn't take her long to overpower me, roll on top of me, and spit in my face.

'That's what I think of you, Pollyanna,' she said. 'And now I have to make it look like Axe Man Antoni killed you. It won't be difficult for the police to put two and two together and realise it was him that did this. I've got information on him and what he did to that Harvey Grant that will put him away for the rest of his life. He's already a killer, it won't be too hard for everyone to believe that he ended your life too. They'll re-arrest him within twenty-four hours after your body is found, I should think. He's bad enough, they probably want to get him off the streets again anyway.'

As I watched my sister walk over to the car, I rolled away and kept moving. *Now was my chance, I was going to get out of this alive, one way or another, and I was going to go and find Danny. Marie had gone mad, that was clear enough. I just needed to get away from her...*

But my feet were still tied together, which was making getting anywhere fast impossible. I managed to stand up and jump away. I opened my mouth and let out the loudest scream I could.

But then I heard the footsteps behind me. I jumped along faster. Then pain sliced through my head, and for a moment I thought my brain had been cut in two. As I fell, I turned and landed on my back. Wetness dripped down the back of my head. Marie was standing over me again. She was holding a large object, one that she'd clearly gone to her car to get. As she brought it closer to me, I could see exactly what it was. An axe. Clearly she hadn't hit me quite as hard as she'd have liked to, because although my head felt like it was splitting in two, I was still conscious...

'So it was you who texted me from that number, telling me not to go to the police. Not Antoni,' I said, as tears began rolling down my cheeks. *Fuck, I was trapped now. I'd fucked up my chance for freedom.*

'Of course it was,' Marie said. 'And have you been feeling a bit woozy today, Polly, after I made you a coffee this morning? I had to drug you, to make sure that you'd lost most of your strength and mind by this evening. It wouldn't have done to have you in fighting-fit form, with what I needed to get done.'

'You bitch,' I whispered. 'You don't deserve my son. He's far too good for you.'

'Apparently not,' my sister said, raising the axe above her head.

'Tell Danny how much I love him,' I said, as quickly as I could.

This blow only just caught the side of my head, but it crashed into my cheekbone and was hard enough to cause me to nearly pass out. I could feel the blood immediately gush from the wound. I couldn't put my hand up to stem the flow. There was no point in trying. My consciousness was going. But I willed myself to stay awake for as long as I could. I was watching my sister bring the axe up above her head again. *I'm going to die now,* I thought. Just as she was bringing it down towards me with all her might, the sound of sirens pierced the air. Then I heard the chop chop of a helicopter somewhere up in the sky.

'Shit,' Marie said, pausing. 'How the hell have they found us?'

Then she raised the axe again and brought it down towards my head. The last thing I remember seeing before the blackness overtook me was my sister turning around and running towards some trees...

Chapter Forty-Seven

'Mummy?' It was Danny's voice. 'Can you wake up now? I've got something to show you.'

My beautiful boy. He was here. I opened my eyes. Well, one of them, the other was stuck shut for some reason...

'Oh, Danny.' I tried to lean forward to hug him. 'You're here. I love you so much, Danny. Are you okay?'

My son was standing next to me. He nodded. He looked paler and a bit thinner than usual, but healthy other than that. I could see now that I was lying on a hospital bed.

'He's doing very well.' It was my dad's thin voice. 'We've both been looking forward to you waking up, Polly. You had us rather worried there for a while.'

I tried to turn my head to find my father, but I found that I couldn't move my neck. I brought a hand up and found that there was a thick brace around it.

'Don't try to move too much,' my father said, shuffling over a bit so that he was in my eyeline, just behind Danny. 'You were hurt very badly, Polly.' I could see that he had tears in his eyes, which was horrible.

'Have I been in an accident?' I said, feeling confused. I

couldn't remember how I'd been injured, only that I'd been wanting to see my son really badly for some reason. I could remember the horrible week in Wales, and the joy of being back in my house in Penge with Danny, and then taking him to Dad's and not being able to find him in the garden, but after that it was just a white mist. Nothing. No memories at all.

'Er, no,' Dad said. 'But I'll wait for a bit to fill you in, if that's okay.' He winked at me, then looked down at Danny.

'Mummy,' Danny said. 'Look at what Grandad gave me.'

He held up a soft white toy puppy.

'I've called him Scamp.'

'Oh, he's gorgeous, Danny.' I gave my son a big smile. I was so, so happy to have him standing next to me. I could feel some sort of big emotional pain in my body start to fade away.

'Scamp has been helping me to look after Danny while you've been poorly,' Dad said. 'Hasn't he?'

Danny nodded.

I tried to move again but it caused a wave of pain to ricochet through my head. I groaned.

I could see a nurse pop her head through the cubicle curtain.

'Oh fantastic, you've woken up, Polly,' she said, coming over to me. 'How are you feeling?'

'Um, I'm not sure,' I said. 'My head really hurts.'

'Well I'm not surprised, with everything that you've been through,' the nurse said.

'I'm still not sure what that is,' I said. I lifted my hand up to feel my left eye. I wanted to work out why it wasn't opening.

'Ah, I see.' A look of understanding washed over her face. 'Your memory's been affected. Maybe you and your dad need some time to have a good chat, eh? Danny, why don't you bring that lovely puppy of yours out here for a bit? We could take him on a bit of an adventure around the ward.'

Panic rose in my stomach. *Danny was going away again?*

'Don't worry,' the nurse said, seeing my expression. 'We won't go far, you'll be able to hear us chatting out here. I'll just take him with me for a few minutes, to give your dad a chance to talk to you.'

I watched Danny leave with the nurse, and then listened intently. Like she'd said, the nurse and my son were still very close to my cubicle. I could hear her ask Danny if him and Scamp would like her to read a book to them. That was okay then, they were still there. Near enough. I looked at Dad.

'Do you remember anything at all about why you're here in hospital, Polly?' he said, taking my hand.

'No,' I said. 'Nothing. My last memory is that we were looking for Danny in your garden.'

'I see,' he said. 'Well, what I have to tell you isn't very nice, but it's important that you know the truth.'

I listened – in utter shock – as Dad told me about what my sister Marie had done to me. How she'd taken Danny from Dad's garden, and then left him with a friend of one of her customers. Apparently Dad knew all about her escorting work now.

'She bought a cheap phone,' he said. 'Used it to tell you that you were in danger, that Antoni had seen police at your house and thought you were snitching on him.'

My mouth was open. It was strange, hearing about such awful events that I couldn't remember, but that affected me so much.

Dad told me all about how my sister had played on the fact that Antoni suspected that I knew about his part in the boy Harvey Grant's murder – Stitches had told her about this in Wales – and apparently she'd told everything she knew about that murder, trying to put their attention onto Antoni.

'In actual fact, it had been Marie who'd seen the police

come to your house that day,' Dad said. 'To ask about a speeding driver. She'd been sitting nearby, fuming. She lured you to a house in Somerset, saying that you were in danger and that she had to hide and protect you. She'd told Sylvie that you were really angry about what had gone on in Wales, and not to answer your phone calls, as you would just be calling to have a go at her and Antoni.'

I wanted to shake my head as I listened, it was all too crazy. But the pain was too much.

All lies, Dad said, but Sylvie – being in the fragile state that she had been – had believed her and hadn't answered my calls. Then while I was in Somerset, she'd drugged me to make me weak, and then phoned me to say that Antoni had found out where I was staying, and was on his way to come and hurt me. She'd told me to run out of the house and up into the woodland around Glastonbury Tor, which – in my drugged-up state – I had done. She'd been waiting for me there, and had then attacked me with an axe. Her plan, apparently, had been to kill me, and then to use Antoni's criminal reputation as a cover, and try and frame him as my murderer.

'But why?' I said through my tears. 'Why would she do all this to me?'

Dad sighed, and even deeper sadness washed over his face.

'Well,' he said. 'After we couldn't find Danny and Marie had mysteriously called you away, I was feeling utterly helpless, as you'd received that text, supposedly from Antoni, telling you not to call the police. I sat there for ages, racking my brains, trying to work out what didn't feel quite right about the situation. It didn't come to me that night, I think I was too tired and stressed to think clearly. But the next day, I started wondering why it was that Marie had phoned you minutes after Danny had gone missing, to tell you about Antoni. Had word really got to her that fast? It all seemed a bit too neat and convenient. It hadn't escaped my attention that Marie's behaviour had become rather strange, and I couldn't forget how angry she'd been when she'd come down from my attic, the day she was so out of sorts at my house. Gut instinct was telling me to go up there, and to try and find whatever it was that had made her so furious. I don't usually go up to the attic nowadays...'

'I know, because your arthritis is so bad,' I said.

'Exactly,' Dad said. 'But that day, I just knew that I had to. It took me ages, but I managed to get up the ladder. And there, on top of a box, was a copy of my will. I must have stored it there several years ago. I know I made several copies and put them in different places, in case I ever lost one of them. Marie must have found it when she was looking for her photos. She must have left it there openly, thinking that it was unlikely that I'd go up there again. As soon as I saw it, I knew that it was Marie who'd taken Danny, not this Antoni character. I phoned the police straight away, and officers came right out to see me. I explained everything to them, how Marie had found the will, then how Danny had mysteriously gone missing, and how I could no longer get hold of you. They asked me for Marie's phone number once they realised that she was probably with you somewhere, and then – luckily – managed to track your location by using the pings that her mobile made off phone towers. *Cellular triangulation*, I think they called it. Very clever. That's how the officers found you that day, and thank God they did. She'd already done enough damage.'

'Jesus,' I whispered. 'What did the will say that made her so angry?'

'That I was leaving all my savings to you, Polly,' Dad said. 'While Marie got the house.'

'Oh,' I said. 'Was that fair, Dad?'

'Yes, more than fair,' Dad said with a grimace. 'Even though Marie has lived such an opulent lifestyle with Henry for years, she's continually asked me to lend her money, which she's rarely paid back. Wealth seems to flow through her fingers like water, she's always had it, but never held on to it. She always asked me never to tell you about the loans. So when I was making my own, new will, after your mother passed away, I decided that Marie had already had a lot of her inheritance, with all the loans I gave her. And you were the one who could actually do with the money, yet you never asked me for anything, Polly.'

I nodded, not saying anything. This was a lot of information to try and digest in one go.

'But clearly, Marie didn't think that this was fair at all,' Dad said. 'When she found the will, her and Henry were going through yet another financial crisis, and I think it was too much for her. Her greed and avarice got the better of her. So she started to think about how she could do away with you, I'm afraid. It makes me sick to actually have to say those words.' He stopped and looked down.

'Because it also says in the will that if something were to happen to you,' Dad went on after a pause, 'then Marie would inherit both the savings and the house. And that was her motivation. It's so sad, what she's become.'

I nodded again.

'Yes,' I whispered. 'It is. Where is she now, Dad?'

'In police custody,' Dad said. 'Where she belongs. I'll always love her, she's my daughter after all. But I'll never forgive Marie for what she's done to you and Danny. Never.'

He shook his head, and a single tear rolled down his cheek.

So my sister, Marie, once so beloved to me, had done all of this. I couldn't get my head round it, yet I could see from Dad's face that what he was saying was true. And his words had triggered flashes of memory to pass through my brain, just transitory images, like Marie's face looking at me as I lay with my hands and feet bound. She did truly hate me. Or did she just love money more? It was hard to tell and right at that moment, I didn't care. I had everything in the world that I wanted, Danny, my dad and my life. Nothing else mattered. My sister wouldn't turn me into a bitter and twisted person, I decided, because I never wanted to become someone like that – full of bile and vitriol, a life-hater who oozed resentment out of every pore. But what she'd done had changed my life forever. I had no idea what the future held, or if I'd ever fully recover from my head injuries. But I intended to live every moment fully, in whatever capacity I could. And to leave Marie behind. I no longer wanted her to have any place in my world. Because despite her best efforts, my sister hadn't managed to take my life and son away after all...

A year later...

'See you in a bit, Dad,' I called to him, as Danny took my hand.

Dad waved back out of his living-room window.

'See you later, you two,' he called out.

A lot had changed since Marie's attack, not least our living arrangements. I'd been in hospital for five weeks, during which time Dad and Danny came to visit me every single day. Marie's attack had left me with permanent brain injuries; there were some memories that I would never get back – both good and bad, which you could say was both a blessing and a curse. Although I'd probably never remember exactly what Marie had done to me that night, enough bits had come back – usually waking me up at night – for me to be able to piece together pretty much everything that she'd done. Bits were missing, and some things had been filled in by the police. But I had patches of memory missing about Danny too, over the last few years. I couldn't remember everything about our holiday at Kilve Beach, for example. Dad had told me that I'd taken my son there, and I'd since read the story I'd started writing based in that location. It hadn't helped bring back memories of that day. Or his fifth birthday party, although I had some photos of it, which would have to do me for now. I couldn't remember doing certain things with Brigitte, although she'd tried to refresh my memory as best she could when she flew over to visit me when I was still in the hospital.

'That time we stayed up all night watching the *Die Hard* films,' she'd said. 'Do you remember that, Polly?' I'd really tried to.

I made an effort not to mind too much about my changed brain, I just had to keep reminding myself that it wasn't important, in the grand scheme of things. And that more and more memories might come back over time.

And my coordination had been affected. I'd also lost the sight in my left eye, as the optic nerve had been damaged by the force of her hitting me with the axe. Luckily, the eye outwardly looked okay now, but I still had wonky vision sometimes, and wobbled when I walked. But these disabilities seemed a minor price to pay for the fact that I was still alive.

We'd tried to get back to normal, me and Danny, after I'd left the hospital and gone to live back in Penge with him. But things never felt right in the house after that; neither of us felt comfortable being there.

'I'm scared here, Mummy,' he would say. And I would nod and hug him, as I knew exactly how he felt. London no longer felt like a safe place for us to live. I realised that what we both needed was a fresh start, in a beautiful place, far away from any bad associations or connotations.

The whole sorry situation ended up bringing Dad and I a lot closer. He was a trooper, coming round to mine every day while I adjusted to my new life with my diminished skills. Luckily I could still type and write stories, not that I was in a hurry to work as a ghostwriter any time soon. And I no longer needed to worry about money, as Dad had kindly released a lot of my inheritance to me early. And for once I knew I needed the help, wasn't too independent to accept his kind gesture. I was so grateful to him for everything he'd done. I was more interested in producing my own work now. And my coordination problems mainly affected my balance, not my fingers.

Dad told me, over the weeks that followed, about how Sylvie had contacted him once she'd heard what Marie had done. He said that she was absolutely distraught and asked for his bank details so that she could transfer me the ghostwriting money that I was owed, which she did as soon as Dad sent them over to her. Sylvie filled Dad in on a lot of things that day, like the connection between my ex, Jakub, and Antoni. They'd been acquaintances for years, she'd said. Antoni would occasionally supply Jakub with some drugs, which he seemed to sporadically use to numb any emotional pain he was feeling. (This was news to me, Jakub hid this side of his life very well.) Apparently the Polish circuit in London was quite tight-knit, and they'd met initially through mutual friends.

Jakub hadn't seemed like a heavy drug user, Sylvie had said, until Antoni got out of prison and started dealing again. Jakub came to him desperate for crack. It turned out that he and his new girlfriend, Christine, were absolutely addicted to the stuff, but as both of them didn't work, they could barely afford any. Hence his desperation for money. Since I'd transferred him the five hundred pounds that Dad had lent me – which thankfully I'd now paid back in full – Jakub had once again disappeared into the background, which suited me and Danny fine. We received the odd text from him, asking how his son was, but that was it. And Danny needed strong men in his life, good role models, and Dad was filling that role nicely, for now. Danny doted on him. Not drug addicts who only cared about their next fix.

Dad and Sylvie ended up getting on really well, and my

lovely new friend came to visit me as soon as she heard that I'd woken up in hospital, and lots when I got out.

'Seeing you get through everything that you have gives me the strength to get my business back up and running,' she said to me one day. She said if I could get through something so horrible, then she could get through a blip in her own life, no problem. I had a feeling that we'd now be friends for life.

With everything that Marie had told the police about Antoni and Harvey Grant, they were able to re-arrest him. When his gang buddies were faced with the prospect of either being charged as accessories to murder, or getting much lighter sentences if they gave evidence against Antoni, they unsurprisingly chose the latter, and he was given a life sentence. So that evil man would be off the streets forever, and Harvey Grant's mum had justice.

I talked to Dad about my idea of moving away for a fresh start, and he said – to my surprise – that he'd been thinking about doing the same thing. He said that living in the house – after Danny being abducted by his aunt from the garden – just felt wrong. He wasn't comfortable there anymore. And he'd finally admitted to himself that his arthritis had got so bad that doing away with stairs and living in a bungalow might not be such an awful idea after all.

'I think I should probably look for a bungalow too,' I said, after he'd told me all this. 'With the balance problems that I have now, I think giving stairs a miss as much as possible would be very wise.'

'Well,' said Dad. 'What kind of place did you have in mind to move to, Polly? What kind of area, I mean.'

'Ah,' I replied. 'I've thought about this a lot, and I've discussed it with Danny. We both want to live by the sea, somewhere really beautiful. In walking distance to the beach.'

'That sounds wonderful,' Dad said.

There was a long pause.

'How would you feel about an old codger joining you in a bungalow nearby wherever you end up?' he said, eventually.

'Oh, Dad, we would love that,' I said. 'What a great idea. It would be so lovely if you moved close to Danny and I.'

So we started looking at potential new homes online, and emailing possibilities to each other whenever we found them. Cornwall seemed to be the favourite; a wild and stunningly beautiful place that was far enough from London to feel like we'd truly got away from the bad times.

One day, when I was perusing a list of houses in Cornwall online, Danny came and looked over my shoulder at the screen.

'That one,' he said, pointing to a bungalow that overlooked the sea. 'That's the one we should move to.'

I clicked on it and we stared at each photo together, both instantly falling in love with the place. It was in Mousehole – one of Cornwall's flatter villages which would be good for Dad and I – and it was a bungalow made from grey Cornish stone, and beautifully decorated inside, with a good-sized garden and fabulous sea views. And the rest, as they say, is history. Dad soon found another bungalow for sale in the same village. Soon both our offers had been accepted. My little house was already on the market, and a family had just made an offer on Dad's for nearly the whole asking price. It turned out that property was significantly cheaper in Cornwall than it was in London, so we were both able to afford our chosen houses, with a good chunk left over. Four months later, Dad, Danny and I had packed up and moved out of London, and were enjoying every moment of settling into life by the sea.

Which is why Danny and I had just waved goodbye to my dad, and were slowly walking back to our own bungalow, which was on a street less than half a mile away. Danny was getting used to the slower pace of life I had to lead now, the way I wobbled sometimes when I walked, and constantly forgot things. He was becoming more patient, holding my hand and slowing his own pace down to match mine.

I'd noticed the change in Danny more when I'd left the hospital and moved back to Penge with him. Dad had tried to warn me that my son was much more withdrawn since the abduction, and that he'd need a good long time to adjust to life with me again. Danny's brief stay with Stitches' sister and her husband hadn't harmed him physically in any way, in fact it seemed that they'd treated him quite kindly, all things considered. But the experience of being taken by his aunt and placed with strangers, and forced to be apart from his mother with no one explaining anything to him, had made him an anxious little boy. He wanted to be by my side at every moment of the day, which was making it difficult to get him settled in the little village school, although we were slowly getting there, baby steps. He slept in my bed every night, and I was fine with that. We'd both been through a horrific trauma, and I'd vowed to do whatever it took to help my son regain that confidence and sense of security that he'd once had.

It broke my heart to see him so changed, but I tried not to dwell on that too much. If I got upset, I just reminded myself that scars – mental, emotional and physical – heal with time. And we were alive and together, and relatively unscathed. We were the luckiest mother and son that ever lived. And I was back to being feisty Polly now. I'd never let anyone walk all over me again, I'd never be a people pleaser just to have an easy life. I was strong inside, despite my injuries. And I knew that Danny would get to that stage too, one day.

Dad had gone to visit Marie once, after she'd been found guilty of attempted murder and sentenced to the maximum penalty – life imprisonment. He told me that she'd been assessed by several psychiatrists, and had been diagnosed as having borderline personality disorder. She'd made herself into the victim of the whole thing, and had berated him for how unfair his will had been. She was unable to take any responsibility for what she'd done to Danny and I. Dad said he wouldn't be able to go and visit her again for a while, but he regularly spoke to her on the phone, and wrote her letters. Poor Dad, he still loved Marie very much. I could see how what she'd done had completely tore him up. I'd decided never to tell him that Marie had been planning to end his life too, there just didn't seem any point in hurting him anymore. She was locked up now and would be forever, hopefully, she could no longer hurt any of us. And Dad was very fragile nowadays, physically. But his spirit was stronger than it had been for years. And there was no way I was going to chance diminishing it again by telling him about my sister's selfish, greedy, money-grabbing plans of murdering him.

I had no plans to visit Marie, although writing to her at some point was a distinct possibility. I'd forgiven her for so much already in life, but I was struggling with her abduction of Danny. I still couldn't get my head around how she'd done that to my son and I, especially to Danny, her own nephew, a small child. It hurt me even more than the axe attack. I didn't hate her, I didn't wish bad things on her, I just needed to keep myself away from her so that I could continue to heal. She was just as much a murderer as Antoni, even if she hadn't succeeded in what she'd tried to do. It had been her intent to finish Dad and I off, and her motive had been pure greed. And in order to accomplish that she'd put me through the pain of taking my son and making it look like Antoni had done it. No, I didn't ever need to see my sister again.

And anyway, I thought – as Danny paused to stare out over the blue-grey waves, before running towards them and throwing a pebble in, watching it splash – I had more exciting things to think about. I'd started running creative writing classes once a week in the village hall, to earn some extra money. And a man with very kind eyes had joined. His name was Stuart, and our personalities had clicked instantly. A few days ago, he'd taken me out for a drink while Dad had watched Danny. Stuart was older than me, divorced and had two teenage daughters who lived with him half the time. He owned a landscape gardening business and was well known and liked in Mousehole; I could tell that by the way that the other writers in my class spoke to him. He liked reading, and he wrote articles for a local gardening magazine. We had a lot in common. We were taking things slowly, very slowly, but I was damned if I was going to completely let my trust in people be destroyed by what had happened with Marie, and with Antoni. I had to keep believing in people. But I was very cautious now. I liked Stuart very much, but it was early days. I wouldn't look too far into the future, or hope for this or that to happen. I'd sit back and enjoy each day as it came. And I wouldn't introduce him to Danny for absolutely ages. Stuart and I were due to meet up again in a few days' time, and I was looking forward to it. And if that went well, then no doubt we'd meet up again and that was good enough for me...

And it looked like my dream of becoming a proper published crime writer might finally be about to come true. In the weeks and months following my return home from hospital, I had a lot of spare time on my hands, especially in the evenings when Danny was asleep. I'd finally signed up for the creative writing course at the Open University, and had been thrilled beyond belief to have been awarded a distinction at the end. When Sylvie had come over for her many visits, we'd decided to give writing her book another go.

'Let's do it, Polly,' she'd said to me, her eyes shining. 'The finished product is going to be better than ever, I can feel it in my bones.'

I was going to write it as though it was fiction, we'd agreed on that, because it gave me the license to go into detail without fear of legal reprisals from anybody. And I already knew her story, had most of it on my Dictaphone. So I set to work, writing it up in the best way that I could. And even though I do say so myself, I think it came out more improved than it did the first time around. We'd decided to include my involvement as ghostwriter in the story, as at that point my life and Sylvie's had become intertwined. So everything we'd been through together was in there; our trip to Wales, Danny being taken, Marie trying to kill me, Antoni being arrested again and charged with the murder of Harvey Grant. Sylvie was absolutely insistent that we put down both our names as the authors of the book; she said it was now my story as much as it was hers. And it felt right to me to do this too. Sylvie had an amazing story to tell, but now so did I. And if we could inspire just one person to carry on through adversity by sharing our experiences, then we'd be happy, we decided.

I sent the first three chapters off to several agents and publishers, together with a synopsis. I'd been through this procedure many times before with other stories, and was used to receiving polite rejections, and I tried to prepare Sylvie for what might be a long road ahead. But then one morning, an email popped into my inbox.

```
Loved the three chapters. Please send
whole manuscript ASAP.
```

It was from the biggest independent publisher in the UK: Blue Reed Books.

I immediately emailed the whole thing off to them, and then

rang Sylvie to give her the fabulous news. She was at her bistro as usual, which was still the thriving business that she'd built up. That was yesterday, and I was trying not to check my phone ten times a minute to see if the publishers had replied. But I had a feeling that everything was going to be okay now, one way or another.

I looked down at Danny, and smiled.

THE END

A note from the publisher

Thank you for reading this book. If you enjoyed it please do consider leaving a review on Amazon to help others find it too.

We hate typos. All of our books have been rigorously edited and proofread, but sometimes mistakes do slip through. If you have spotted a typo, please do let us know and we can get it amended within hours.

info@bloodhoundbooks.com

Printed in Great Britain
by Amazon